TEA FOR TH

Stories by
Candis J. Graham

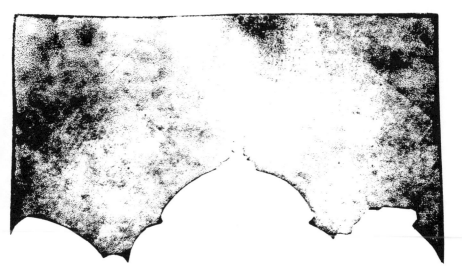

Im*pert*inent Press

Earlier versions of the following stories have been
previously published:

"A Second Time," *Lesbian Bedtime Stories II*, Tough Dove Books,
October 1990.
"O Mother," *Furie Lesbienne/Lesbian Fury*, Vol. 4, No. 2,
December 1987.
"She Just Feels That Way," *Fireweed*, Issue 28, Spring 1989.
"Bir," *Common Lives/Lesbian Lives*, Issue 25, January 1988.

Published by
Impertinent Press
Box 23097, 2121 Carling Avenue
Ottawa, Ontario, Canada K2A 4E2

Cover design by Watermoon Design Inc.
Cover photo by Wendy Clouthier.

Printed and bound in Canada.
First printing 1990.
Second printing 1991.

Canadian Cataloguing in Publication Data
    Graham, Candis J. (Candis Jean), 1949-
        Tea for thirteen

    ISBN 1-895349-00-1

        1. Lesbians–Fiction. I. Title.

PS8563.R3145T43 1990   C813'.54   C90-090562-X
PR9199.3.G73T43 1990

This book is dedicated to my mother, Margaret B. Graham.

She taught me to read, although it seemed a hopeless task, and then took me to the public library.
She gave me books and still does.

Acknowledgements

So many poems I read are
dedicated to or written about
famous women. I wish I could
write poetry. I would create
poems about the women who are
famous to me, for I am blessed
with the friendship and support
of some grand women. Although
I am naming only a few here,
each woman is precious.

Gu'n robh mìle math agaibh.
(A thousand thank yous.)

Bev Curran for her superb editing and her commitment to
lesbian culture.
Brenda Landry for always asking about my writing and for her
excitement.
Claire Piché for inspiring "With My Little Eye".
Gabrielle Nawratil for her interest in everything and the intense
lunch conversations.
J. A. Hamilton for her letters, advice, and encouragement.
Joan Bridget for her laughter and sensibility.
Lise Corbeil Vincent for reading everything with enthusiasm and
asking for more.
Marie Robertson for believing in me all along, and for sharing
her lesbian passion.
Mary Staples for inspiring "Modern Illusions".
Wendy Clouthier, *ionmhuinn*, for her love and wise words, and
for the magnificent house on Blackburn.

And thank you to my father, Kenneth J. Graham (1917-1990),
for supporting me in whatever I wanted to do–even when it didn't
make sense to him.

Thank you:
Fireweed and The Women's Press for recommending me to the
Ontario Arts Council for grants in 1988.
House of Anansi, *Quarry*, and The Women's Press for
recommending me for OAC grants in 1987.
Donna Quince and Maxine McKenzie for providing me with
opportunities to read at House Works from 1986 to 1989.
The women at West Word Two (August 1986 in Victoria) for
urging me on and for the many moments of ecstasy.

Contents

A Second Time

I went dancing, after weeks of thinking about it.
I knew that I had to get out and meet new women.
But I'm never comfortable in crowds, even crowds
of dykes. Still, it's better than being alone every
night.

I found myself sitting with some women I knew
by sight. That's when I spotted her. I guess the
woman beside me noticed her too.

"She has quite the reputation."

I turned. "She does?"

"Yes," the woman said. "She's here every week.
She's always alone. She was involved with a
woman for years, three or four for sure. They split
last spring."

I watched her walk across the room, winding
her way around tables and clusters of women. I
said nothing to the woman beside me. The band
had taken a break and the silence was heavenly.
Not silence, really, but women's voices rather than
loud music. The heavenly sounds of women
talking and laughing.

She stopped to talk to someone. After a brief

conversation, she resumed her trip across the huge room. She walked slowly, with a lazy stride, as if she had all the time in the world.

I couldn't resist asking, "Do you know her?"

The woman beside me lifted her glass mug of beer. "Kind of. I know about her." She drank from the mug, knowing she had my attention and deliberately taking her time. "I know her name." She took another drink. "Her name's Erin."

It suited her. Erin. The perfect name for this woman with short short hair and over-sized purple glasses. Erin of the lazy stride.

"She sleeps with everyone."

My mouth fell open. I turned. "How do you know she sleeps with everyone?"

She gave me a pitying look. "Everyone knows."

Everyone knows she sleeps with everyone. Everyone! Rumours. Innuendoes. Gossip passed from woman to woman, and presented as fact. Don't we relish the distorted details, speculating about the lives of one another. It entertains us, as long as it isn't about us.

"Yes, she has quite the reputation." There was a sense of satisfaction in her voice.

My fury astonished me. I wanted to scream, wanted to yell at the woman beside me, wanted to shake her. Erin sleeps with everyone, does she! Well I'd bet money that she was celibate, that's what I'd bet, that's how much faith I'd put in idle rumours! I ignored my inner voice and asked, "Do you want another beer?"

The woman beside me smiled. "Sure."

I walked away quickly. I had no intention of getting her a beer. She could faint from thirst before I'd get her a beer. I wanted a beer myself, so I headed for the bar.

I joined the line-up, standing behind Erin. I hadn't planned this. I was thirsty. I'd watched her walk in the direction of the bar, true. But I was only here because I was thirsty.

I wasn't angry anymore. I felt excited to be standing close to her. I looked down at the floor, trying to calm my racing heart. She was wearing bright yellow running shoes. I have a friend who says you can tell a lot about a person by her shoes. Do women who wear yellow running shoes sleep with everyone? I almost laughed out loud.

"Why are you smiling?"

I looked up. Erin was grinning at me, waiting for my answer.

"I had a funny thought, that's all."

"What were you thinking?"

Her eyes were looking into mine, warm hazel eyes behind the glass, inviting me to look back. Usually I am tongue-tied, especially around women I admire, but words came easily. "You wouldn't be amused. Trust me."

She laughed. "Try me."

It was her turn at the bar. She ordered mineral water with a slice of lemon and produced the correct amount of money from a purple pouch on her belt. I was in a state of panic, afraid she would walk away. I ordered my beer and called after her.

"Wait!"

She turned, still grinning.

"I'll tell you."

She laughed again. "I can't wait."

I took my beer from the counter. "Come out here, in the hall where it's quiet."

She followed me. She was following me! My heart was thumping. What could I say to her? She would not be pleased if I said I'd been told that she has a reputation for sleeping with everyone. The band started playing loud, energetic dance music as we left the room. Maybe I'd ask her to dance, after I'd figured out how to explain why I was smiling at the bar.

The hall was deserted. We stopped in an alcove beside a water fountain, and I turned to look at her, to see if those hazel eyes were still warm and inviting.

She bent forward and kissed the end of my nose. "I couldn't resist. Do you mind?"

I shook my head, speechless. She kissed my nose. What did it mean, that she kissed my nose?

"Why were you smiling back there? You said you'd tell me."

I nodded. What if it was true, her reputation? What could I say to those hazel eyes. No lies. The truth is, the truth...

She leaned toward me and put her lips on mine, warm lips, my heart pounding, open lips, searching tongues. I wanted to shout for joy. I wanted to hold her close to me.

"I've missed you," she whispered.

I put my arms around her, trying not to spill any beer and wishing the mug would vanish into the air. "I've missed you, Erin."

"So, why were you smiling?"

I moved back a little to look at her. "I was thinking your yellow runners should be scarlet, to match your reputation. Did you know that you sleep with everyone? That's what I've been told." I hadn't meant to blurt it out like that.

Tears filled her eyes. Wet hazel eyes. She was always able to express her emotions as she felt them. I'm more inclined to control my feelings. I moved her close to my body again.

"I sleep with myself!" She cried the angry words against my shoulder.

"I thought so." Her smell was just as I remembered. A hint of soap and freshly-ironed clothes. "Let me put this beer down so I can hug you properly."

"You never do anything properly."

I grinned. "Wanna dance?"

"I have missed you."

I felt warm all over. "Me too. Let's dance."

She took off her glasses and wiped the tears from her eyes and cheeks with a forefinger. "You want to dance with a scarlet woman?"

"I'd be honoured."

She laughed, put her glasses back on, and reached for my hand.

Berries

Leah had the radio on while she ate breakfast. She was eating a healthy meal and listening for the weather report. It was not a generous breakfast. Generous, ha! One poached egg, one slice of toast made from wholewheat bread, and a small, very small, glass of real orange juice. Skinny food. No, not skinny food, skinny portions. She'd rather have two eggs, three pieces of toast, maybe four pieces, with raspberry jam, a heaping portion of fried potatoes and onions, tomato wedges, at least six or seven crisp curls of bacon. *That* was a generous breakfast.

She cut the egg carefully into tiny pieces. Cholesterol wasn't skinny. Just another word for fat. Chunks of yellow fat clogging her veins. Or was it arteries? But one egg every few days, one egg from a free-range chicken wouldn't do any harm. It was protein. Protein was healthy. A body needs protein.

Thirty pounds. She dipped a corner of toast in the puddle of yellow yolk. Starting today, she had to lose thirty pounds. She had it all planned, had been planning for months. She bit the corner and then licked her lips to catch stray crumbs. She was going to be careful about what she ate and how much she ate. That was the secret. Small quantities and no carbohydrates. That was how she'd lose the weight.

The woman next door said the way to lose weight was to eat slowly. "If you eat slowly," Muriel insisted, "you get full before you can eat too much. You give your body time to let you know to stop eating before you've had too much." Her neighbour lost eleven pounds that way. It took five months. At the end of the five months Muriel and her husband went to Boston for a week to celebrate. She came home weighing six pounds more.

Leah had decided to eat slowly, as well as being careful about how much and what she ate. It couldn't hurt, and maybe it would help. She needed all the help she could get. Losing weight was going to be a battle.

She took a small bite of toast and chewed slowly. Everyone had a theory. Her mother said the trick was to drink two glasses of water before each meal. "The water fills you up," her mother said, "so you eat less."

Every theory involved eating less and feeling hungry all the time. Losing weight meant looking at food and thinking about food that must not pass through her lips. Somewhere there must be someone with a theory that would allow her to eat more, insist that she eat more as a way to lose weight. Foolishness. She took a large bite of toast and chewed slowly. Food in her mouth meant weight on her body. It was that simple. Food equaled pounds.

Leah looked down at her thighs. Two glasses of

water before every meal would go directly to her thighs. Everything that passed through her mouth landed on her thighs. And on her hips and her belly. And her breasts and her face. What did her mother know about it, anyhow. She weighed a hundred and twenty pounds, soaking wet! But everyone, simply everyone had a theory about how to lose weight, and everyone was willing to give advice.

"It's eight thirty-four with a high of twenty-eight and showers later today. Don't forget your umbrella!"

Rain. She reached over and switched off the radio. Two weeks of sun, non-stop sun, sun every blinking day, one hot sunny day after another, and today, today of all days, it was going to rain. It wasn't fair. The very day she planned to pick berries.

She used the teaspoon to scoop up three tiny pieces of egg white and chewed slowly, savouring the taste and the texture. She looked down and inspected her thighs. She'd never be skinny. Who was she trying to fool. Nothing worked.

Jean said she liked large women. She said some bodies weren't meant to be skinny. Jean didn't say skinny, she said slim. She said, "Some bodies aren't meant to be slim. Some bodies, like yours, are meant to be voluptuous."

Leah liked that word, voluptuous. It sounded warm and sensual. Voluptuous, ha! Models for Van Gogh and Rubens, they were voluptuous women. But that was centuries ago. It was different now. Fashions had changed. Slim was in. And she was fat, f-a-t.

She hated that word. Fat. When others said it aloud, she could hear the disgust in their voices.

She didn't want to be fat! What could she do?

Jean had no use for those weight-loss places. She said losing weight had become big business. It was fashionable to be skinny, fashionable to fork over money to big corporations that specialized in diets and other humiliating tricks. Jean said they hired abnormally skinny women to promote their weight-loss programs. The women dressed in designer clothes, always dresses, never pants, with their earrings matching their necklaces, and belts and high heels that matched their purses, and they knew the secrets of applying make-up. Leah liked it when Jean said they were *abnormally* skinny women. These abnormally skinny women took money from large women and shamed them into obsessive behaviour. Like counting calories and eating peculiar combinations of food. That's what Jean had to say about it.

But Jean wasn't fat. Jean was skinny. Jean was s-l-i-m.

Her neighbour had tried one of those places. For three months she had watched every morsel of food that went into her mouth. Twice a week Muriel dressed in her good clothes and visited the weight-loss office. She lost nine pounds that time.

"Ten cherries equals one apple," she informed Leah one afternoon, as they stood at the bus stop. "I'm gonna keep at it, but it sure takes a lot of willpower to eat ten cherries and not one more."

It was hopeless. Leah would never look like those abnormally skinny women. She couldn't afford the smart designer dresses anyway. She laughed, and drank the orange juice, having saved the best for last, tipping her head back, closing her eyes, blocking out everything except the taste of sweet oranges. Then she rinsed the glass and plate under hot water and left them in the sink, on top of the cast-iron frying pan and beside three dirty mugs. Jean wouldn't care if she came home to a messy kitchen. It was a source of constant amazement to Leah, the disorder that Jean could tolerate. Tolerate, ha! She wouldn't even notice the piles of dirty dishes. How could she not notice? That was a mystery.

What would she wear to pick berries? It was going to be a scorcher today, even if it did rain. The beige shorts were too tight, had felt snug since last summer. That was sad, because they were her favourite shorts. Her very favourite. She'd liked them from the moment she saw them in the store. And then, when she tried the shorts on, she knew she had to have them. The back pockets had flaps which concealed her ass.

Ass. That was her mother's word. Another of those hateful three-letter words. Move your ass. She always heard a silent 'fat' between 'your' and 'ass.' Ass was one of *those* words, like fat. There was a sound of disgust, she could hear it, when people said ass.

She stood in the doorway of her closet, staring at the row of clothes. Jean said she didn't mind Leah's size, but Leah couldn't believe that. How could anyone not mind? No one liked fat women. No one, not even the fat women themselves. Skinny was beautiful. Skinny looked good in two-piece bathing suits, in scrimpy bikinis, in tight jeans. A fat ass looked good in nothing. No matter what Jean said about voluptuous.

Why did she keep the beige shorts? She couldn't wear them anymore. She should give them away so someone else could get pleasure from them. But no one would ever feel the pleasure she had felt. She was never going to lose weight. She'd never fit into them again. Never. Never ever ever. Shit.

It mattered most in summer. In winter, she could hide under layers of clothes. But in summer, ha! In summer, the temperature rose and as it went up people took off their clothes. All that exposed flesh was indecent. Even at work, where she expected people to dress modestly, it was work, didn't they know, they wore as little as possible. That skinny woman at the other end of the floor, she wore Bermuda shorts. To work! Scrimpy bodies in scrimpy clothes.

She reached for the black shorts with the tie waist. They made her feel like a sack of potatoes with a rope around her middle. But they were comfortable, and black was a secretive colour, concealing her shape. The tie waist didn't bind, the way the beige shorts did. But she couldn't wear shorts. Shorts would expose her thighs. And her bare legs would get scratched by the branches. Scratched fat flesh.

She frowned and moved into the closet, reaching for the white trousers. They were stained with paint, from the summer before last when she and Jean had painted the back porch, so it wouldn't matter if they got dirty. They used to be too big. She had bought them for the soft cotton, subtly patterned, soft, so soft, knowing they were too loose, yet not caring. That was before. Now they fit. They were even a little snug, around the hips especially. But she wouldn't feel exposed in them.

She stepped back to survey the closet. Everything was neat and orderly. Short-sleeved shirts, long-sleeved shirts, winter trousers, summer trousers, sweatshirts, t-shirts, shorts, vests, jackets, each had a section of the closet. But nothing fit!

The phone rang. She placed the white trousers across the foot of the bed and reached over to the telephone on the bedside table. It was Bonnie, wondering when Leah would pick her up. Leah frowned and assured Bonnie that she would be there in twenty minutes, thirty at the most, depending on traffic. She hung up and raced around, putting more effort into getting ready than she felt capable of in the heavy humid air. Summer. It was muggy and she could barely breathe, as if a scarf was wrapped around her face and blocking air to her nose and mouth. It would be cooler in the country.

The white pants were tight around her waist and belly and hips, tighter than she remembered. She couldn't have put on more weight. Were they tighter? Or was it her imagination? There, there was a blob of paint, over the knee, the same blue as the back porch. It looked like a solid chunk, ready to be chipped away in one whole piece. She picked at it but it didn't budge.

She chose a short-sleeved sweatshirt. It was over-sized, stretching down over her ass to her thighs. A cover-up. She turned from side to side to see herself in the mirror, then stopped, face forward. The bright yellow shirt billowed around her. Did it make her look even larger? Voluptuous, ha! A stern face glared back at her.

When she arrived at Bonnie's house, Bonnie was sitting on the front steps, reading a book. Bonnie always had her nose in some book or other. Jean said there must be something wrong with a woman who read so much. Maybe Bonnie couldn't cope with reality and had to hide in books. Maybe she was afraid of real people. Jean was always coming up with theories to explain people's behaviour.

"She's shy," Leah explained to Jean. "She just likes to read. She goes to the library every Saturday morning."

"A *bookworm*," Jean said, making it sound like an infectious disease.

Jean's attitude puzzled Leah. Jean was a kind soul. But not towards Bonnie. Leah wondered if Jean was jealous of their friendship. Sometimes, not too often, once every few months, Leah and Bonnie went to a movie, one that Jean didn't want to see. Nothing for Jean to be jealous about, but then, jealousy wasn't a logical emotion. But what did Jean have to worry about? Women didn't fall all over themselves to get to know fat women. It pleased Leah a little, that Jean might be jealous, might think another woman could be interested in her.

Bonnie stood up and waved. She was wearing a tank top and short shorts. Wouldn't you know it. Short shorts! Skinny toothpick arms, bony legs. Skinny all over. Even a skinny chest with tiny breasts, almost invisible breasts, under that tight top. Leah waved back and brought the car to a stop. She looked down at her own ample bosom. Bosom. That's how she thought of her breasts. Bosom, ha! It was a word from an older generation, before her mother's time. Large breasts were fashionable back then. Women were supposed to be voluptuous. No more. That time was over. Now it was the starved look. Twiggy, in the sixties, she started it all. All bones, that woman was, all bones. No softness. All points and angles and hard bony surfaces.

"Hi!" Bonnie made herself comfortable in the passenger seat. "Do you think it'll rain?"

"The radio said rain for this afternoon. Have you got the seat belt? It looks like rain. See those clouds?"

"I hope it doesn't rain. I've been looking forward to this all week. I'm glad you asked me to go with you. I've never picked raspberries."

Leah turned the car onto a busy street. Bonnie chatted but Leah heard only bits and phrases from the monologue. She concentrated on driving. It was a relief, all in all, to have to focus on driving. She knew she ought to listen to Bonnie. But it was hot. Sticky hot. The waist of the white trousers was binding her. Maybe she should have worn the black shorts. Traffic was heavy. She'd thought there wouldn't be many cars at this time of day. Rush hour was over. The back of her sweatshirt was damp with sweat, and the shirt and her back were sticking to the plastic seat. A tank top would be cooler. But a tank top with these breasts and the rolls around her middle. Shit.

As soon as they turned onto the highway, large drops of rain plopped on the windshield.

"No!" It was an involuntary cry. She had hoped that if she refused to believe it would rain, then it wouldn't rain.

"What is it?"

Leah was touched by the concern in Bonnie's voice. "The rain."

The rain stopped, as suddenly as it had started, and the sun shone again.

"That's not the end of it. Look at those dark

clouds." Bonnie pointed. "Have you been to this
farm before? Is it far?"

"We're nearly there. Jean and I pick strawberries there every year. Her mother freezes them."

"Do you pick raspberries too?"

"Last year we did. Jean made two raspberry
pies. She's very fond of berry pie. She taught
herself how to make pie crust so she could make
the pies. Her mother froze the rest, but they didn't
turn out as well as the strawberries."

"I'm going to make cheesecake. I've never made
raspberry cheesecake."

Leah switched on the car radio. Country music
blared out. Bonnie would make *cheesecake*. All
those calories. She'd most likely eat the whole
thing by herself and never gain a pound. A pound!
Never gain an ounce would be more like it.

Nothing was fair. If she so much as looked at
cheesecake, why even thinking about cheesecake
could do it. Calm down, and concentrate on
driving. Foolishness, thinking she could gain
weight by looking at food. Plain foolishness.

"Can we get baskets there?"

Leah turned down the volume of the radio.
"What did you say?"

"Will there be baskets there? I don't have
anything to put the berries in."

"I brought baskets and some rope. We can tie
the baskets to our waists and free both hands for
picking."

"What a good idea!"

Leah smiled. Bonnie would see, when they got
there, that everyone did it that way.

"You're making jam? How much do you need?
Have you made jam before?"

Why was Bonnie talking so much? She was

usually quiet, saying little. She sure was in a gabby mood today. "I need two litres, whatever that is. I haven't adjusted to metric, but the recipe's in metric. This is my first time making jam. Have you made jam?"

"No. My mother used to make jam, all kinds. And other preserves, dill pickles, relish, beets. The best was her peach jam."

"I love peach jam. We're here. That's the farm." Leah turned right, onto a dirt road.

The huge parking lot was almost empty. Leah noticed a few people in the fields, close to the barn. She opened her door and looked up. Heavy grey clouds were moving overhead. The radio had said rain this afternoon. If only it would wait, hold off for a few more hours, until she had her raspberries.

"Let's hurry and try to beat the rain." Even as she spoke, she knew it was hopeless. Those were rain clouds. It was going to pour, soon, any minute now.

They took the baskets and rope from the trunk and reported to the field supervisor, a skinny, tanned youngster of seventeen or eighteen. She directed Leah and Bonnie to two rows of berries, half a city block away. As they walked, Leah showed Bonnie how to tie the basket around her waist. There was rope left over, dangling from the knot at her waist. Before she tied a basket around her own waist, Leah undid the button at the waist of the white trousers, looking over to make sure Bonnie wasn't watching.

She handed Bonnie a second basket. "Leave this one on the ground while you pick. When that one is full, switch baskets. You take this row. I'll take the next one."

Leah started picking. She ignored the scratchy brambles, moving quickly along the row. Sounds of other voices, neighbouring pickers, annoyed her. One man whined about the cost of someone's wedding, and speculated on the private habits of various relatives. His voice carried in the country stillness. It was hot. Hot and muggy. Whew! Bugs, too, making more noise than rush-hour traffic. The country was supposed to be peaceful.

"Leah! How do I know which ones are ripe?"

The bodiless voice hung in the heavy humid air. Leah paused, then backed away from the wall of vines and projected her voice up and over the top. "The ones that fall into your hand as you touch them, they're the ripe ones. Taste a few. You'll know and you'll see the difference in colour."

She resumed picking, wondering if she had given bad advice to Bonnie. Surely the berries were sprayed with insecticides. Wasn't everything sprayed these days? The berries should be washed before entering a mouth. She crouched to reach a cluster of ripe berries. She could feel her trousers stretching, pulling at her hips, straining as if the material would tear. They couldn't tear. They were made of good cotton, expensive material, the kind that has long strands and lasts for years. It was her imagination. If she shifted a little, put more weight on the other leg. There, that was better. She could eat a few berries herself. But that wouldn't erase the bad advice. Insecticide in two stomachs, instead of one.

She stood up abruptly. Her armpits were wet with sweat. The weight of the basket, almost full of luscious berries, was dragging at her waist. She shifted the rope a little and inserted two fingers in the waistband, trying to loosen the material.

Everything was too tight. None of her clothes fit. But what was the point in spending more money on new clothes when she was going to lose weight?

Was she going to lose weight?

It started to rain as she exchanged baskets, carefully placing the full one beneath some overhanging leaves at the end of her row. The raindrops were gentle and the cool water felt refreshing against her hot skin.

"Leah! It's raining."

"Yes. I noticed." A drop landed on her forehead and slid slowly down the side of her face, like a lonely tear. It had to rain, today of all days.

She resumed picking, moving slowly. The field was quiet. Everyone else had left. No voices, even the bugs were silent, no sounds, nothing except her breathing and the sound of tranquil rain. She picked a plump, ripe berry and put it on her tongue. Sweet and soft. She crushed it against her cheek with her tongue.

The jam recipe called for two litres of berries and one litre of white sugar. Two to one. A gigantic mound of sugar. Sugar that would cling to her thighs and inflate her belly, her breasts, her face.

"Leah! Are you there?"

"Yes, I'm here."

"It's quiet, all of a sudden."

"Yes, it's peaceful, isn't it. Are you getting lots of berries?"

"I'm getting wet."

Leah looked down. "Me too."

The wet yellow shirt was clinging to her body, revealing mounds of breasts and belly. Her wrists and hands were covered with tiny red scratches. Slender wrists. Skinny wrists. Somehow, her wrists and ankles were immune to food. Or whatever it was that put this weight where it wasn't wanted. Tiny raindrops dripped from her hair and slid down her back, making her shiver. The rain had cooled the air. She was moving quickly now, berries from hand to basket. She wanted to stay all day, picking mountains of berries, smelling the musty earth, working alone with no sound except the gentle rain.

She paused to push wet hair away from her eyes. There, at eye level, was a miniature breast. She laughed out loud. What a rude thought. But it did look like a breast, a raspberry breast, a breast without skin.

"Leah! Is that you?" Bonnie's voice sounded thin, almost weak.

"Yes, it's me." Her own voice sounded loud and clear. The voice of a full-bodied woman. She laughed again. She had a full-bodied voice and a full-bodied laugh. "It's me, Bonnie, laughing to myself."

"Do you want to go soon?"

"Yes, sure. In a minute."

Metabolism. That's what it was. Slow, fast, eager, bored—bodies are controlled by metabolism. She was meant to be fat. She was intended to be a large woman, a magnificent F-A-T woman. Leah put her basket on the ground and bent down close to the wet ground. The earthy smell filled her nostrils. She wanted to stay here forever, close to the earth, sheltered by the raspberry vines.

Could she ever be skinny like Bonnie? If she stuck to the diet, if she ignored her hungry stomach, could she do it? Did she want to? She licked a large cool raindrop from her arm. Could she lose thirty pounds? Could she shrink to the

size of a skinny woman? She'd try. Shit. She'd try!
And she'd keep the beige shorts. Maybe they'd fit
next summer.

Would the beige shorts fit Bonnie? No, never.
Bonnie's a skinny minnie. She'd swim in them.
Swim, ha! She'd drown in them.

Leah laughed. No, now, calm down. She smiled
and put a lush, plump breast in her mouth.
Delicious. She had done all this herself, picked all
these delicate berries, enough raspberries for
raspberry pie. And she would make jars and jars
of deep red jam, enough to last all fall and
through the winter.

O Mother

I look up from the novel I am reading and she is standing before me. She is ready to go out, dressed up by her standards.

"Where's the funeral," I ask, and wish I could take the words back as soon I hear them.

"O Mother," she moans through dark red lips. "Does this shirt look all right with the skirt?"

I bite my lip as I study her. I gave her that black shirt for her birthday, against my better judgement. Doesn't every shirt go with jeans? The blue eye shadow matches her jean skirt. "Yes. You look stunning."

"O Mother!" She comes over and hugs me. "See you later."

Her hug is a bribe, a request for tolerance and silence. Lately she gets angry when I ask where she is going, what she will be doing, when she will be home. I'm her mother. I need to know what she is doing. I can't be bribed. "Where are you going?"

"Over to the shopping centre." She is frowning at me.

"Supper's at five. See you later, Jesse, spelled J-E-S-S-E."

She laughs. "O Mother."

When she is gone, I stand at the kitchen

window and watch her walk down the street. The jean skirt is too short. She's getting tall. She's almost as tall as I am.

She was a gorgeous baby, plump and cheerful, with fine blonde hair that made her look bald. I know all mothers say that their babies are beautiful. But mine really was. I used to sit and watch her for hours on end.

I'd bathe her every evening just before bedtime. Someone told me a bath would relax her and help her sleep. After the bath I'd wrap her in a large towel and sit with her in front of the mirror. We'd play games. I'd count her fingers and then her toes. One toe, two toes, three toes, four toes. Then, this little piggy went to market, this little piggy stayed home, this little piggy had jam and bread.

Sometimes I'd tickle her. She'd giggle and laugh and kick her tiny dimpled legs. I'd always tell her she was beautiful. See the beautiful Jessie in the mirror. Aren't you a beauty, so strong, yes you are, you're strong. Kick those strong legs. Look at those powerful arms. My darling baby. And I'd kiss the top of her head. I loved the smell of her and the feel of her small round body against mine. Then I'd diaper her, put on a terry-cloth sleeper, and read her a story. She always fell asleep while I read. I knew those stories by heart.

It wasn't easy, working all day and going to the child care centre to get her on my way home. I was always tired. I thought life would be easier when she was older.

We fight every day.

My daughter has changed her name. She's fifteen now and it's a difficult age for both of us. Some times are better than others. It's pretty bad at the moment, bad enough that I've been wondering if sixteen could be any worse. That kind of thinking can lead to serious depression.

One day her clothes are skin-tight from the waist down and baggy from the waist up, the next day her clothes are baggy from the waist down and skin-tight from the waist up, and the next day everything she wears is too tight and too short. She's fond of hot pink and bright green, often together, although most of her clothes are black.

I have to keep reminding myself that times have changed. When I was growing up children never wore black. It was a colour reserved for new widows and older women, for women much older than I am now.

She's always worn her hair long. Last month she had it cut and what's left is an inch long all over. Her friends have this short hair style too. And what her friends do is more important than anything else on this planet. I like her with short hair. It shows off her beautiful face. But it's one more change and there have been so many changes lately.

She is part child and part adult. It comes of living with me, just we two, and being around my friends. She is amazingly comfortable with adults, much more comfortable than I was when I was a teenager. I can tell that sometimes she is laughing at us. We think we know so much more than she does, but she is not fooled, not for one minute. She's an expert on life and we are old women, past it.

She's turned the corner and disappeared from sight. Is she going to meet Ted? I was afraid to ask.

I gave her a beautiful name. Jessie. She's changed it to Jesse. It sounds the same when you say it out loud. Jessie. Jesse. But she's concerned with more than mere sounds.

"Jesse," she informed me last week, "looks more sophisticated. Classier. You know? It's kind of elegant."

"Classier? Elegant?" I said, leaning against the cupboard with my hands in hot dish water, watching her dry the salad bowl. My strong child. "You don't need that eye shadow and lipstick to be elegant."

"O Mother," she said with a half smile.

I said, "I guess Jesse's more androgynous."

"O Mother," she said, shaking her head.

Silly me. She isn't interested in androgyny. She wants to be a woman, in the *femme* sense of the word. She shaves her legs and underarms and plucks her eyebrows and paints her fingernails blood red, and drowns herself in some cheap perfume called Passion or Desire which would more appropriately be called Overpowering.

I don't think she really understands the meanings of those words. Not at a feeling level. What can a fifteen-year-old know about passion or desire?

Perhaps I am wrong. The desire in her to be sophisticated and elegant is a powerful emotion. It's driving both of us crazy. Perhaps I underestimate the depth and intensity of her feelings.

"Mum, I have a boyfriend. Kind of," she said as she put the salad bowl in the cupboard, her back to me. "His name's Ted."

A boyfriend? My baby has a kind of boyfriend? She can't be serious. I've got to say something. What can I say? Say something, anything, before she turns around and sees my face.

"Is he in your class?"

"No. He's in Ewa's class."

"What's he like?"

"He's okay."

He's okay. We used to have long conversations about everything and nothing. Now it is an effort for her to speak more than five words to me at one time. This isn't how I imagined it would be between us.

Could she be meeting Ted at the shopping centre? What's he like, this okay Ted? Who is he? Is he the reason she's changed her name?

She always liked her name. People often comment, what a pretty name, or, what an unusual name. It makes her feel special. But special isn't enough anymore. She wants to feel sophisticated and elegant.

She's even changed my name. For fifteen years she's called me Mum. Suddenly I have become O Mother.

I'm trying to be understanding. Fifteen is, after all, a difficult time. She needs my support. Someday I will become Mum again and she will be Jessie. I have to believe that. This is a period of transformation for her, from child to adult. We will both survive it.

I remember what it was like to be fifteen. Sixteen was even worse. And seventeen...well, I prefer not to remember. I've never been one of those people who wishes she could be eighteen again. When I hear someone say that, I am horrified.

It's frightening to think this stage could last a few years. How will I get through it?

There are times when I want to grab her by the shoulders and dig my fingers into her skin and shake her thoroughly. Shake her so hard that her brain cells will rearrange themselves and she will become a reasonable child again.

It's a vicious thought. I have all this anger and I don't know what to do with it. I'm not really angry that she's changing her name and my name. I feel hurt because she is no longer my child. She is becoming her own woman. And she's battling me every inch of the way.

I love her name. I debated about what to name her all through the pregnancy. I wanted to give her the right name. I liked Lisa and I liked Colleen. If she was a boy, it would be Sean or John. But as soon as I saw her I knew she was Jessie. All the other names flew out of my head. Jessie was the name for her. No middle name. I am a practical woman and middle names serve no useful function.

A name is important. It's how we identify ourselves in the world. She looks like a Jess, with her friendly smile and assertive walk.

Her name is really Jessica. I call her Jess and sometimes Jessie. When I think about it, she has three names already. Now she wants a fourth one, Jesse.

That's not what makes me angry. I'm angry because she is rebelling against everything and mostly she's rebelling against me. She wants me to be like all the other mothers. It's a Hollywood fantasy, fed by t.v. shows that bear no resemblance to real life. I'm not like t.v. mothers. First of all, I'm a lesbian. There isn't so much as one t.v. show with a lesbian mother.

A few weeks ago she said she couldn't bring her friends home anymore. "They're not stupid," she said. "They'll know."

"Know?" I was bewildered. "They'll know what?"

"O Mother. There are never any men here. Just women!"

How do I cope with raging lesbophobia in my own daughter?

Second of all, she wants to be like t.v. daughters, in all their feminine regalia. Make-up, bra, dresses, panty hose, heels. And she criticizes me for not wearing any of it.

I never expected this. I brought her up in a feminist home, brought her up to reject those props, to question everything. I brought her up to be proud of being female, to love herself and respect other women.

There's no third of all. My being a dyke and her being a rebellious *femme* female are enough.

That's not true. There is so much happening here. I am her mother, having cared for her all these years, named her Jessie within minutes of her birth, fed her from my breasts, taught her to tell time and eat spaghetti with a fork and spoon. I've lived with her all these years, three hundred and sixty-five days a year for fifteen years. Five thousand and four hundred and seventy-five days. Not counting leap years. That's a long time. So where did she learn to feel shame about her mother the dyke? I never brought her up that way.

And the nights, five thousand four hundred and seventy-five nights. Nights when she was sick. Lonely nights of worrying about her, was I doing it right, this bringing up a child. Such an odd expression, to bring up a child. What else do you bring up except vomit?

I've tried to do everything right, to give her all the love and attention she needs. Sunday afternoons we'd sit at the kitchen table and draw.

I read somewhere that kids should be encouraged to be creative and that a colouring book only teaches them to keep within the lines. I wanted a daughter who wasn't limited by lines.

We'd each take a large sheet of newsprint and share the box of crayons. Sometimes we'd copy the illustrations from her library books. Sometimes we'd draw each other. Sometimes we'd create pictures from our imaginations. One day we drew our hands. I framed Jessie's drawing of her left hand and put it beside my bed.

She'd ask questions while we worked. What are the crayons made of? When will it be Christmas again? How do they get the toothpaste in the tube? Why is it green? Where does snow come from? Some questions I couldn't answer. I bought an encyclopaedia, a book a month through instalment payments.

Afterwards we'd tape our drawings on the inside of the front door. I'd take down the ones from last Sunday and fold them carefully before putting them in a box, which I kept in the hall closet. We'd tape the new ones to the door and then make pancakes for supper.

I still have those drawings, three boxes full.

I am her mother. But I am not important anymore. She is rebelling, struggling to be independent, bound and determined to find her own place in the world. I'm frightened. Sometimes I don't know her. Will we ever be like we were?

I'll make myself some tea, then sit down and hem her new skirt. Perhaps I'll make pancakes for supper. We haven't had pancakes in a long time.

She has a boyfriend named Ted. Why does this bother me, when her girlfriends never bothered me? Does he tell her that she looks beautiful?

Does he tell her she is strong? But I mustn't make a big deal out of it. I have to keep my sense of humour.

I'm trying. I left a note for her yesterday.

> Dear Jesse
> I've gone shopping. Be home by 4.
>
> love
> O Mother

She was not amused. "Really Mother," she muttered when I got home.

I can't bear the thought of becoming Really Mother.

She Just Feels
That Way

Cait opened her eyes. Patterns of sunlight danced on the far wall. That pleased her and she smiled, a sleepy half smile. She wanted the cheery influence of a sunny day to help her get through the meeting in Ottawa.

She had been worrying about the meeting for days. Dealing with bureaucrats was not easy under the best of circumstances. It looked hopeful this time, though. The government woman, Francine, had been receptive during their telephone conversations. More than that, she had been friendly and helpful. Francine was not a decision maker, but she seemed to have some influence. And now the feds were paying Cait's way to Ottawa, for this meeting, to discuss the funding proposal.

The bureaucrats had to approve the application for funding. Everyone at the office was working long days and feeling constantly exhausted from trying to get all the work done. Burn-out was the word everyone muttered lately, as if saying it aloud would change anything. Cait knew the only way to improve the situation was to close the office for a month and give the women a chance to rest. But that would be a short-term solution. A long-term solution would be to hire more staff.

Closing the office would mean abandoning so many other women. All their clients would be left to fend for themselves. It was an impossible situation. The funding application for two additional staff women would make the difference. The feds had to approve it.

Would it be sunny in Ottawa? She turned over and lifted her head and shoulders just enough to see the alarm clock. It couldn't be 8:45. There wasn't much time. She had to leave for the airport by ten. It was going to be a busy day... she yawned...the end of a busy week. She bent forward and kissed Heather's forehead.

Heather smiled and reached out to put her arms around Cait. Without opening her eyes, without saying a word, Heather pulled their bodies together. Cait watched Heather's sleepy face as their bodies touched, sharing warmth, limbs tangled. She freed a hand and rubbed the small of Heather's back.

Heather opened her eyes and kissed Cait, looking into her eyes as her tongue stroked Cait's teeth. Cait curled her lips against Heather's lips, returning the pressure.

Heather pulled away and propped herself up on one elbow. She looked down at Cait, reaching out to brush away stray hairs from her face. The loving gesture made Cait smile. She moved her hands under the bedclothes, tracing the outline of Heather's body, along her curving hip, down her long thigh, over bony knee, pausing to stroke the thick growth of shin hair.

Heather ignored the roving hand. She put one hand on Cait's shoulder and pushed her onto her back. Lifting her own body over Cait's, she lowered herself, looking into Cait's eyes, resting her breasts on Cait's breasts, brushing her pubic hair back and forth across Cait's curly black pubic hair.

Cait forgot the Ottawa meeting. She watched the contours of Heather's face, her long nose, fine cheek bones, rounded chin. The meeting of pubic hairs excited her. The familiar features of Heather's face reassured her, and her nipples hardened.

She put her hands on Heather's round rear and pulled downward, pushing, pressing pubic bones and hair. A vision of brilliant red poppies filled her mind, a field of silky petals quivering in the breeze.

They kissed eagerly, with open mouths, Heather resting all her body weight on Cait. The warm pressure of Heather's body made Cait want to laugh out loud. She curled her feet around Heather's ankles and pushed upward. Pressing her body hard up against the length of Heather's body, she laughed and the poppies vanished in a cloud of pink dust.

Their tongues danced for one another and Cait imagined a waterfall, frothy water cascading downward in an endless rush. She moved, sliding her hips sideways against Heather, and Heather joined the rhythm. The motion intensified Cait's lust. Tumbling water, falling, pouring into a busy stream, swelling, surging forward.

Heather moaned, a slow sound from deep in her throat, and Cait felt the sound against her cheek bone. She hugged Heather fiercely. She saw a sander, gliding over the surface of a table, and she could feel the vibrations in her belly, up and down her thighs, along the lips around her vagina.

"What are you thinking?"

Cait opened her eyes and saw Heather's smiling blue eyes. "I was thinking of a sander. I felt the vibrations and I can still smell the sawdust."

Heather grinned, looking like a mischievous small girl. "Hot sex makes you think of sanding wood?"

"What were you thinking?" Cait asked, sounding defensive to her own ears.

"Don't get uptight. I love your extraordinary imagination." Heather bent down and kissed her. "I was thinking about the smell of your body."

"Eau de sawdust?"

They laughed together. Heather reached down, parting Cait's pubic hair gently before sliding two fingers into her wet vagina. Cait caught her breath and held it, slowly closing her eyes. Heather's fingers stirred, around and around, then in and out, making Cait moan softly.

In Cait's mind, Heather was preparing soup, stirring the ingredients in their shiny soup pot, her muscular arm moving, mixing, circling, round and round. She felt Heather's tongue...wet circling her nipple, round and round, over and around, teasing, tempting her to ask for more direct touch. She wanted touch, not talk. All she could think of was Heather's tongue and fingers, fingers beating at the mouth of her vagina, gentle pounding, then sliding in and out. She had to give some of this feeling back to Heather.

She slid her left hand over the arc of Heather's bum to the crease. All four fingers stroked up and down, pausing to caress her small opening. One finger, the longest one, pushed at the anal opening, forcing in, one fingertip buried in the snug hole. Heather cried out, an involuntary noise, and bit Cait's nipple. The cry echoed in Cait's mind and a rush of joy made her fingertip push harder, delve deeper, downward, into Heather's delicate body. Heather tried to move away, forcing more weight against Cait, but the fingertip was firmly lodged. The fingers in Cait's vagina slowed and then moved quickly, urgently, in and out, in and out.

Then the fingers were gone, leaving Cait breathless and empty.

Cait's fingertip moved slowly in and out, gradually slipping deeper with each movement. Heather's fingers brushed over Cait's congested labia lips, kneading lightly.

"Softly, easy," Heather murmured against the side of Cait's face. "I like that."

"Two fingers?"

"No," she said quickly. "One's enough."

Heather's fingers moved up to Cait's clitoris. Their breathing was noisy, a harmony of excitation. Cait concentrated on the sound of breathing and imagined the sound of gentle rain, the steady patter of water drops hitting leaves. A rhythmic, rapid sound. She felt Heather's fingers massaging her clitoris, spreading heat, and wanted to scream the pleasure that filled her body.

"More! I want more." Cait opened her eyes.

"As much as you can take!" Heather laughed and smothered Cait's breasts with tiny moist kisses. She bent down to bury her face in Cait's belly, all the while caressing Cait's clitoris with her fingers. Cait watched Heather and her mind was filled with music, fingers playing piano keys, lively fingers creating loud sounds. A melody of wild emotion. She wanted to weep.

Heather moved away abruptly, releasing Cait's fingertip from her anus, and bent her head over Cait's pubis. She slid a hand under each of Cait's buttocks and nuzzled her face in the silky pubic hair. Cait closed her eyes and it seemed that her heart paused for a moment. Then the tongue touched her, releasing her heart beat. She moaned and moved both hands to the back of Heather's head.

The alarm went off, making shrill noise bounce around the room. Both women hesitated before separating. Cait opened her eyes as Heather's warm body moved away. She watched Heather crawl to the foot of the bed and reach out to stop the racket.

Heather turned to look at her. "It's nine-thirty. What time do you have to leave for the airport?"

"Ten, at the latest. And I have to iron my shirt, check my notes, and phone the office." Cait stretched, then curled into herself, dragging the crumpled bedclothes up over her body.

"You don't seem like a woman who leaves what she starts."

Cait looked at Heather before answering, trying to gauge the tone of her voice. "I'm running out of time. I'd like to stay. Heather, you know I want to keep going, but this meeting is important."

Heather lay beside Cait, stroking the length of her body through the bedclothes. "I'll make breakfast while you shower." She sighed, loudly.

"You're a dream."

"I'm real." Heather laughed and sat up, looking at the shape of Cait's body beneath the bed-clothes. "And so are you."

Cait giggled. "Don't I know it. Come here. Hold me. Let me hold you."

"Are you sure you have time?" Then Heather threw herself on top of Cait and buried her face in Cait's shoulder.

"Shall we continue when I get back tonight?"

"I'll be waiting." Heather lifted her head and smiled. "A day of anticipation!"

They both rushed around the house, getting Cait ready for the trip. Cait was preoccupied as she prepared for the day ahead of her. But once she was on her way, sitting on the plane and waiting for take-off, she remembered Heather's hands. She felt warm hands tracing patterns on her body and smiled to herself, then turned her face to the window to hide her secret smile from the other passengers. She looked up at the clouds and the blue sky and saw waves of warm water, crests of white foam, soft hands rolling over her body.

A man stopped at her row and made a fuss as he shoved his briefcase under the seat, folded his raincoat and threw it into the overhead container, and rammed his newspaper in the pocket of the seat ahead. He seated himself, dropping his full weight onto the seat beside Cait, and adjusted the back of his seat. His restless activity distracted Cait from her thoughts. She turned to look at him. He was yanking at the seat belt, trying to make it stretch across his suit into the matching connection. A grey suit, charcoal grey.

She propped her elbow on the arm rest between their chairs, claiming her right to use it, and rested her chin on her hand. On flights between Toronto and Ottawa the majority of passengers were men in suits. Even when she flew late at night, there were men in grey suits, men in navy suits, occasionally men in brown suits. Each one carried a briefcase and often a garment bag. They sat, looking self-important in their look-alike suits, reading *The Globe and Mail* and eyeing the flight attendant. They always seemed well-fed. Like this one, with a round face and fleshy neck skin bulging over his tight collar.

And there would be more of them, like this man, at the meeting. Well-fed men in grey suits and navy suits.

Cait looked down at her own suit. Trousers, in the colour called teal green this season, a misty pink shirt, and the jacket was cream and teal green in a tiny plaid pattern. She had bought the outfit at Simpsons, especially for this meeting, to show the bureaucrats she was a respectable woman so they would loosen the purse strings and dip into their bag of funding money. It was a small concession, wearing smart business-like clothes. Was it necessary? Playing their game by their rules, to get what she wanted?

She brushed her hand along the trousers, enjoying the feel of soft wool. She deliberately wore trousers. Their rules called for skirts, but she wouldn't give in on that one. The other women at the meeting would be wearing dresses. She'd bet her whole pay cheque on it. They always wore dresses. Was it because they thought they had to wear a dress to be dressed-up? It continually amazed her to see women wear skirts, showing panty hose legs. The world was as it should be: women in dresses and men in grey suits.

The man beside her cleared his throat. "Do you mind if I smoke?" The cigarette was already in his hand.

Those minutes with Heather this morning had made her late getting to the airport, so she had to accept a seat in the smoking section. "No," she said, looking into his eyes. "It's your funeral."

He looked startled. Cait turned to the window to hide another smile. It made her feel better, feel less anxious, to be assertive with him. In a dark corner of her mind she was uncomfortable with all these men. Why couldn't the plane be filled with women wearing suits and carrying briefcases? Better still, women wearing a variety of clothing and carrying flowers?

Cait took a taxi from the airport to the high-rise government building. She sat in the back seat, stroking the left knee of her wool suit and watching the city. It was an overcast day and looked like it would rain at any moment. As the taxi moved slowly through downtown traffic, she yearned for a cup of hot tea. She had tea on the plane, but it was lukewarm and served in a styrofoam cup.

Francine, the friendly woman of the phone calls, met her at the security desk. They shook hands. Cait noticed Francine's grip was firm and that she looked into Cait's eyes.

"How was your trip?"

"Fine, thanks. I've brought the information you wanted."

Francine smiled. "Very good. We'll have time to go over it before the meeting. The meeting's been delayed. An unexpected question in the House has two of the people running around."

She escorted Cait to the elevator and up to the tenth floor, through a noisy warehouse-like area of endless desks and wall dividers, into a windowless room containing chairs and a coffee table.

"We can review everything here, until the others are ready for the meeting. Please, make yourself comfortable. I'll be right back."

She left Cait and returned in a few minutes carrying a tray with a pot of coffee, cups on saucers, white plastic spoons, tiny square paper napkins, a small carton of 2% milk, and packets of sugar. As Francine placed the tray on the coffee table, Cait noticed an ornate gold and silver wedding band on Francine's ring finger. She was disappointed.

"Do you have tea?"

"No. Sorry." Francine frowned. "Everyone here drinks coffee. One cup after another all day long. It keeps us awake."

Cait laughed and accepted a cup of milky coffee, wondering how anyone could drink this stuff all day long. Francine poured herself a cup of coffee and they started to go over the funding proposal line by line.

On the second page, Francine looked at Cait and said, "To be quite honest, we're not going to be able to fund the clerical position. Our mandate is to promote research and policy development."

Cait took a deep breath. "We know that. But the clerical and secretarial work is essential to the operation of the office. Someone has to open the mail and answer the phone and file the research and type the policies! To add a research position without a clerical one is a nightmare."

"Yes, I know the work is essential. I started out as a secretary. But our guidelines are clear and there isn't any way around it. I've been fighting them on this for you. I've gone to bat for you. But I don't believe the Chair of our committee will budge."

The door opened and a man poked his head into the room. "Francine, Mike needs you."

Francine turned to Cait. "Excuse me. I'll get back as soon as I can."

Cait sat alone, drinking cup after cup of milky coffee, staring at the funding proposal. What could she do? Was it possible to convince them in spite of their guidelines? What could she say to make them provide funding for that position? It would be a wasted trip if they didn't. And morale at the office would suffer.

She tucked her hand in the pocket of the wool jacket, making a tight fist. A fist to delight Heather's wet vagina. She imagined an open window with sheer pink curtains blowing in the wind. A fierce wind howling and pink curtains flapping back and forth urgently, while Heather kissed her and held her body, all of her, safe and warm in Heather's strong arms.

An hour later Francine returned, saying, "Sorry. I apologize for the long delay. We're ready to meet now."

She led Cait through the warehouse of desks to a meeting room on the opposite side of the building.

Francine introduced Cait to the five people. During the introductions, Cait was careful to shake hands firmly with each person and make eye contact. Everyone seated themselves at the oversized table and the meeting started. Two men wore grey suits, one wore a navy suit, and one wore a brown tweed jacket with brown pants. Francine was wearing a shirt-waist dress, in the colour they called pumpkin this season, and the other woman wore a silky white blouse with a grey skirt and navy jacket.

"Although you do not usually fund clerical positions, this part of the proposal is vital to us." Cait paused for a moment, and looked slowly around the table at each face. The man in the navy suit cleared his throat and looked down at the papers before him. "This work is vital to any office. And, as you know, part of our philosophy is to help women gain skills to move out of clerical work. The woman in the clerical position will work closely with the research position and gain skills." She paused again and looked around the table. Before she could continue, one of the grey suits spoke.

"Yeah. But we don't do that and..."

The brown tweed jacket, the Director, interrupted him. "You make your position clear in this proposal. It's a well-written document. Your group has a good reputation. We'll discuss it with the finance people next week. Let's not worry about that right now. I have some questions about the budget."

What did he mean, not worry about that right now?

The grey suits criticized other parts of the funding submission, but Cait knew their concerns were minor. As the experts, as the ones with the money, they had to demand changes. They couldn't wholeheartedly approve of something proposed by a non-government organization. They took turns talking, seeming to enjoy the sounds of their own voices. The brown tweed jacket occasionally asked a question, always to clarify something in the proposal. His questions were short and to the point.

Cait happened to look at Francine, as the grey suits and the navy suit argued about the work schedule for the research position. Francine winked at her and grinned. Surely that meant they'd fund the clerical position. She'd won! And Francine had done it, had gone to bat for Cait and somehow she had managed to convince the Director that the position was necessary.

Cait looked back at the arguing suits. She smiled politely and nodded, noting each of their comments in her notebook. Her heart was singing, We have the money, we have the money, everyone will be excited, relief is in sight, we have the money. She wanted to throw her arms around Francine and kiss her. Thank you, Francine, her heart sang, Thank you.

After the meeting, Francine escorted Cait to the security desk and called a taxi for her.

"You've done it. He'll find a way."

"No, you did it. Thank you, Francine. Every woman at the office and all our clients will pray for your health and happiness tomorrow, when I tell them."

Francine laughed. "I'll phone you next week and let you know the details."

They shook hands and Cait said, "That's a beautiful ring."

"Why, thank you. It was my grandmother's. She gave it to me when I turned thirty and I've worn it ever since."

Cait sat beside the window on the return flight, holding some long-stemmed flowers she had bought outside the air terminal. This time a woman took the vacant seat. Cait smiled at her, a white-haired woman wearing jeans, then relaxed back into the seat and pictured Heather meeting her at the airport. Heather would greet her with a hug and a kiss on the cheek, always the right cheek. She would be surprised and pleased to receive the purple irises and orange tiger lilies. She might give Cait another kiss, on the lips, right there in public.

Once the plane was airborne, Cait stared out the window. The moon was full and bright, lighting up the sky like the fabled star of Bethlehem. She followed the plane all the way to Toronto, and Cait watched her. She wondered if Heather knew it was a full moon. Yes, Heather would know. She was a moon woman, observing the phases, preferring when it was full because they could make love with the curtains pulled back and moonlight filling the room, shining on their bodies.

She watched the moon until she lost sight of it when the plane circled, prior to landing. They could do that tonight, pull back the curtains and let moonlight into their bed. She could almost feel Heather's fingertips on the back of her neck, her lips on her shoulder, her teeth...she felt the wetness in her underpants and smiled.

Modern Illusions

Glenda is enjoying her solitude. It's Sunday evening, the end of another weekend. Soon enough, tomorrow morning at seven forty-five when she steps onto the crowded express bus and travels downtown, she will return to the world of people.

She is planning a spring party. Glenda takes small bites of a sandwich, Hungarian salami on wholewheat bread with a light coating of prepared mustard, and chews slowly. It's a comfortable home, she thinks, as she looks around, admiring her possessions. In a short while, at eight, she will turn on the twenty-inch colour t.v. and watch a murder mystery while she irons. It is part of her Sunday evening routine. She irons while she watches the murder mystery, then she changes channels and watches two half-hour British comedies on the public t.v. station. She irons slowly, but not carefully. She has trouble understanding accents and misses half the jokes on the British shows, but comedy is her favourite kind of t.v. show and there's nothing else worth watching at 9 p.m. on Sunday.

As she looks around, she has an idea that pleases her. She will buy flowers for the dinner party and sit them on the library table. A pot of yellow tulips or perhaps a dozen red roses. She will buy both, if she is feeling rich that day. If not, just the yellow tulips. They'll look perfect for the party, yellow tulips against the warm wood of the table.

She uses her thumb to wipe bread crumbs and mustard from the corners of her mouth. Yellow tulips and red roses will make the room feel warm, will make it look genteel, will be the perfect touch for a spring party. It is a splendid idea. Spring flowers on the table.

The library table, refinished yellow birch, is her special pride and joy. Of all the furniture she has accumulated over the years, this table is her very favourite. It was the first piece of furniture she bought after she graduated from university and had a job. In those days, good-paying jobs were easier to find.

She found the table at a flea market. She liked it the moment she saw it. The longer she stood there looking at it, the more she wanted to take the table home with her.

"Buy it," her friend Miriam said. "It's a bargain at that price. I'd get it, but I just bought my sound system and I don't have a penny to spare for the next few months."

She paid forty-five dollars for it, borrowing a twenty-dollar bill from Miriam. She was excited as she and Miriam struggled to fit it in the back seat of Miriam's Mustang, finally turning the table over and resting it, upside down, on the seat.

She started refinishing the table immediately, in her almost empty one-bedroom apartment, using fine sandpaper and a commercial chemical stripper recommended by her father. She lived happily with the fumes as she stripped away layers of paint. Removing years of paint and stains and dirt took many long hours over a period of weeks. Eighteen years later, she still finds herself stroking the surface from time to time, delighting in the feel and sight of the table.

Now the table sits near the front door of her two-bedroom apartment, with her favourite books, the ones she reads over and over again, lined up on the shelf between the two legs: the diaries and novels of May Sarton, the novels of Edith Wharton, the novels and autobiographies of Han Suyin, English translations of Colette's novels, mysteries by Margery Allingham and Dorothy L. Sayers, and the novels and edited diaries of Virginia Woolf. She does not have a complete collection of the words of any writer. She is content to own the books which are her favourites.

Beneath the table clumps of bluish-grey dust rest in a harmless fashion on the shiny oak hardwood floor. She turns her head to examine the other side of the room. There they are, more balls of dust gathered casually along the floorboard. She usually ignores the dust balls. Where do they come from? It is as if they have a life of their own, starting out as tiny specks of dust and then suddenly growing and multiplying and spreading randomly throughout the apartment. It would make, she thinks, a great plot for a feminist science fiction novel. *The Mutiny of the Dust Balls.*

She chews the last mouthful of sandwich and looks around the room, avoiding the floor area and the possible discovery of more communities of dust balls. But she cannot avoid them. Now that she looks at the room through the eyes of her friends, the dust balls are a source of shame. And she knows the large clumps of dust are a sign. They mean the whole apartment needs cleaning, needs hours of work with a powerful vacuum cleaner and buckets of hot, soapy water.

Glenda has never owned a vacuum cleaner. When she was much younger, newly-graduated from university and installed in her first apartment, she used to vacuum once a week religiously. In those days, she had a different image of herself as a woman. To be a woman meant cleaning her home, meant devoting hours each week to eliminating all signs of dust and dirt and disorder, meant making mirrors and taps shine.

She borrowed vacuum cleaners, borrowing also her father's car to lug the equipment to her apartment. From this she learned that all vacuum cleaners are not equal. The best one was her mother's Electrolux. Its powerful sucking action easily surpassed that of the Filter Queen belonging to her friend Miriam and the pitiful Kenmore she borrowed, in moments of desperation, from the woman downstairs.

She knows what needs doing, but through the years she has done less and less. There are many reasons and sometimes she makes a mental list, to justify the soap-caked bathroom sink and sticky kitchen floor. But ultimately the real reason, the reason at the top and the bottom of her mental list, is that she has changed. She no longer needs to vacuum and dust and scrub to feel she is a good woman. Her image of herself as a successful woman is more closely tied to her

job, which she refers to as her career, and her
friendships, and the years of consciousness-
raising she has gone through, the politics she
has acquired about the status of women, and her
relationships with her family. Not necessarily in
that order, she thinks and smiles to herself. She
bites into the second sandwich.

She knows what needs doing, but she refuses
to force herself to do it. The floors need washing.
The tiles on the bathroom walls need a thorough
cleaning with a strong disinfectant. Lately she
has noticed a mildew smell in the bathroom. The
smell distresses her when she is in there, but she
forgets about it the rest of the time. The shower
curtain needs to be washed. The bathroom mat
needs to be washed. The window and the curtain
across it need washing. The toilet bowl needs to
be scrubbed and disinfected.

When she views her home through the eyes of
her potential guests, it becomes a shabby and
shameful place. She sips apple juice from a
highball glass and looks around the room. She
has learned to live with the dust and dirt,
although she tidies the disorder from time to
time.

Her friends, all women concerned with their
careers and the status of women, have also
changed through the years. But she believes they
have managed to maintain a devotion to
housecleaning. Certainly, whenever she is invited
to their homes, the dust balls have been
efficiently removed. Their bathrooms smell clean
and look scrubbed. Every room is tidy to the
point of looking barren and unoccupied, like
hotel rooms or model homes in new housing
developments. Well, not quite that barren, she

concedes to herself. But nowhere are there piles of magazines and unopened junk mail. She never sees stacks of dirty dishes beside the kitchen sink, chairfuls of unironed clothes in the bedroom, and rumpled towels in the bathroom. Unlike hotel rooms, her friends' homes are filled with plants and the plants always look healthy.

Still, she has decided to have the dinner party, decided a few weeks ago to organize it for this month, decided she needs to do something to welcome spring and renew friendships. After months of dark evenings and unstable weather, which produce a mild claustrophobia in Glenda, she yearns to break loose. She deserves this party and she will have it. All that is left to do is decide on which friends to invite and which menu to prepare.

But something will have to done about the dust balls. How? She does not have time. And anyway, even if she had time she does not want to waste hours on her hands and knees washing floors and trapping dust balls. It bores her. It tires her. She does not have time.

She could pay someone to do it. This flash of inspiration pleases her, and she feels able to lift her head and look around the room again. It is the perfect solution. She will find someone to come in one morning while she is away at work. She likes the idea. She will leave a messy apartment in the morning and come home to a sparkling clean home. Why hasn't she thought of it before? It's the perfect solution. Not only for the upcoming party, but forever. If she can find someone to come in, say every two or three weeks for a few hours. That should do it. That would be sufficient to keep her home clean and free of the tenacious dust balls. No longer would she have to ignore the dust balls along the floorboards and the grubby ring around the bathtub.

Her first doubt appears a few minutes later, while she is ironing and watching the murder mystery and planning the menu in her mind. She is thinking about serving purple grapes with cheese, Camembert and old Cheddar, before the main course and wonders if there is still a boycott on Californian grapes. She will phone Miriam after the murder mystery and ask. Miriam will know. She subscribes to lesbian magazines and feminist magazines and labour magazines. Miriam always knows what is happening in the world.

Glenda decides to tell Miriam about the inspiration to get someone to come in and clean.

Her first doubt follows that thought. How could she ask another woman to do her dirty work? How could she ask another woman to do work she won't do herself? What will Miriam think of her? She imagines Miriam will be horrified by the idea and will think Glenda oppresses other women. She is ashamed of the inspiration and, in the next moment, is ashamed of feeling shame. Their friendship, twenty years old, has survived many disagreements and a few misunderstandings. They have developed a tolerance for one another, an acceptance, and even many moments of mutual admiration. She feels safe with Miriam. Miriam will understand.

But if she can't hire a woman to clean the apartment, what will she do about the dust balls?

She raises the question when she phones her friend after the murder mystery, as the first British comedy starts. Miriam has an answer.

"I never thought of it that way, that it oppresses

women, but if you feel that way, get a man to do
it. A woman cleans my house. She's a refugee
from Vietnam and doesn't have any other
marketable skills. She needs the work and she's
good at it. She keeps my house spotless. But you
could hire a man. I've seen an ad in *Gay Times*
by a man who does housecleaning."

"A man? I don't know. A man doing house-
work? I've got the latest issue. I'll look for the ad."

She thinks, as she puts away the ironing
board after the second comedy, how odd it was
that she hadn't known someone else cleaned
Miriam's house. Did any of her other friends have
women clean their homes? Odd, too, that no one
ever talks about it. She had assumed they did
their own cleaning, sporadically, when it became
unbearable or before entertaining friends. Or
perhaps secretly, as part of their weekly routines.

Then she sits with a pad and pen to list the
party guests, and watches the news.

Glenda is pleased with herself a week later,
another Sunday evening, when Clive is sitting on
her couch. The menu is planned. She has
invited all her favourite friends. And now she has
someone to clean the apartment.

It has been a busy day. Brunch with Miriam.
An unexpected visit from her nephew to ask if he
can borrow her camera and tripod for a school
project. Telephone calls to and from family, and
telephone calls to invite friends to the party. She
is tired of people and hopes Clive will leave soon.
The murder mystery is going to start. She has the
ironing to do. He seems to be business-like in his
approach, moving to the matter at hand after a
few pleasantries about the weather.

"I charge fourteen dollars an hour," he says, looking around the room. He looks back at her. "What do you want done?"

She hands him a sheet of paper. The list reads: vacuum, dust, tidy closets, clean fridge, wash floors, clean bathroom, lemon oil on wood surfaces, wash windows.

Will he know she means vacuum under the bed and under the rads and in the closets? Will he know she means clean the bathroom mirror and inside the cabinet beneath the sink? Should she have put more detail on the list? Will he do the ironing too?

"How much time do you think it will take?"

He studies the paper. "Five hours, maybe longer. The first time will take longer because the place hasn't been kept up."

She decides to ignore his comment. It is the truth, but she thinks he is rude to say it aloud. "There's a problem, though. I don't have a vacuum cleaner."

He smiles, his first smile since entering the room ten minutes earlier. "That's a first. I've never met a woman who didn't own a vacuum cleaner." He studies the paper again. "I could bring mine, but I'd have to take a taxi both ways and charge you."

"Okay. Can you start this week?"

"Sure. I can do it tomorrow afternoon or Saturday morning."

"How about Saturday morning? I'm having a dinner party that evening and I'd like the place to look perfect."

"Sure. There's something you should know first. I hope it won't make a difference." He looks directly into her eyes. "I like to wear women's clothing while I clean."

Glenda is startled and uncomfortable, but quickly brushes her feelings away. She looks at the lifeless grey t.v. screen and says, "No problem. How you dress is your business."

After he leaves, she stands in the middle of the living room watching the murder mystery and ironing, thinking about this man who likes to wear women's clothing and imagining what she will tell her friends. It will make a great story for the dinner party. Won't they laugh as they raise their glasses in a toast to the end of winter.

She'll tell them about her need for help around the place, laughing, Don't the dust balls get out of control if you don't have a firm hand? But who has time. And then she'll tell them about her flash of inspiration. Hire someone to do the cleaning. She'll confess her reluctance to oppress another woman. Although she supposes some women like that kind of work, and some women can't get any other kind of work, and for some it means being self-employed and independent. So she hired a gay man to clean her apartment. It was all Miriam's idea, isn't Miriam a wonderful idea-woman, a good friend. But it turns out he likes to dress as a woman while he cleans. Imagine that! Isn't it a laugh, a double role reversal, a man doing housework but dressing as a woman to do it. Surely there's something profound there.

It'll bring the whole issue of housework out in the open and her friends will reveal how they keep their homes so clean and tidy. She imagines her friends laughing, and saying to one another later, Isn't that Glenda something. So avant-garde, hiring a man for a cleaning lady.

She thinks about Clive all week and finds herself wondering what he will wear to clean her apartment. The thought preoccupies her, even at work, in the classroom where she teaches secretaries to use DOS and WordPerfect.

She tries to picture the slender man in a full-length red sequinned gown and black patent heels. And then in a pink party dress over a starched crinoline with pink velvet pumps on his feet. Will he wear jewellery? Pearls. Or imitation diamond earrings and matching bracelet. Will he shave his legs and wear panty hose? He'll have to, in that getup. And heels, he'll have to wear heels. His collar-length hair is too boyish for full drag, so he'll have to wear a wig.

She can imagine him in a white satin gown, the shiny material clinging everywhere, over false bosoms and padded hips. He'll wear white satin stiletto heels that have a little bow on each toe, and a large white satin bow at the back of his blonde wig. She favours the white satin gown. No one could clean a toilet wearing a crinoline. It would be impossible, impractical, absurd! And sequins, they'd catch on everything. Will he arrive all dressed up? Or will he use her bathroom to change?

Why would anyone dress as a woman to clean? Surely even a woman wouldn't wear a dress to clean. She turns the question over and over in her head, trying to make sense of it. Yet it does make sense to her, in a strange sort of way, that he would wear traditional female clothing while performing what is usually regarded as women's work. She considers other kinds of women's work and tries to picture male nurses in starched white dresses with crisp caps on their heads. Something about that image bothers her, although she can't figure out what it is.

And, as she keeps reminding herself, it is really none of her business. What matters is how he does his job, not how he dresses. Can he do the job? Should she have asked for references?

As Saturday approaches, she wonders if she should be friendly, invite him to have a coffee and a little conversation with her when he arrives. Will he misunderstand? Will he think she is lonely, desperate for conversation and looking for a friend? Or maybe trying to overcompensate for her discomfort about his dress? Will he consider it part of his work time and charge her for it?

Friday night she makes a decision. She has to go out Saturday morning to buy the flowers and some pistachios which she has decided, at the last minute, to add to the menu. She will invite him to have a coffee. Then after ten minutes or so she will get up and leave to do her shopping.

Clive arrives punctually at nine. He is wearing faded blue jeans and a corduroy bomber jacket. He is carrying an Electrolux vacuum cleaner with various attachments and a plastic shopping bag, yellow plastic with LOBLAWS in thick black letters.

"Do you shop at Loblaws?" She is curious about the contents of his small plastic bag. It is too small for a starched crinoline, too small for a wig and gown and heels.

"No. I don't know where I picked up this bag." Clive lowers the vacuum cleaner to the floor, gently placing the attachments beside it. He keeps the plastic bag in his left hand.

"Would you like some coffee before you start?"

"No. Thanks. I'd like to get going. I'll stop for a coffee in a few hours."

"Okay. I have to go out to do some shopping. I'll get out of your way."

"Good."

As she pulls a bright purple sweatshirt over her head, she wonders what he means. Good that she is leaving? Good that she will be out of his way?

"Bye. See you later."

"Goodbye." Before she closes the door behind her, she notices he has placed the plastic bag on her library table.

The florist at the shopping centre has a perfect pot of yellow tulips, the flowers just beginning to open. The price is fourteen ninety-nine, which she calculates quickly in her head to be over sixteen dollars with tax. As she pays for them, having decided she can't afford to buy red roses as well, not when she must pay Clive seventy dollars or more, she wonders what he will be wearing when she gets home. A short cocktail dress. Something that fits easily into the plastic bag, a short dress in a light delicate material with spaghetti straps. Perhaps he has a short-haired wig. One that can be rolled into a small hairy ball to fit in the plastic bag with the dainty cocktail dress.

She looks down at her own blue jeans. She's a woman and she doesn't own a dress. But at this moment, someone in a dress is cleaning her apartment, a *male* someone in a dress. And then she remembers make-up. She almost laughs out loud. He must wear make-up. Was there room in that small plastic bag for make-up too? Lipstick, mascara, eye shadow, blusher, eye liner. She does not wear these things herself, but she was brought up to be a woman and she is familiar with them. Surely dressing like a woman would mean wearing make-up.

Will he wear false eyelashes? No. No one wears false eyelashes anymore. Except perhaps a man in drag. Cross dressing. That's what they call it these days. Cross dressing when men wear dresses, but not when women wear trousers and ties.

She carries the pot of tulips carefully in the crook of her right arm while she finishes shopping. As she walks past the familiar stores, she remembers that this is the only mall in the city which refuses to allow volunteers from the local association for the mentally challenged to set up a table to sell their Christmas cards. The company which manages the mall justified its position by saying the association would be competing with the retail stores that sell cards. Each December she goes out of her way to visit another shopping centre, one which allows the association to set up a table, to buy three packages of their Christmas cards. The cards are boring and do not rival the ones sold by the stores. She buys them anyway because she wants to support the association. And each December she thinks about boycotting her regular shopping centre. She really should. But she never does. It is convenient. It is within easy walking distance of her apartment. It has a good bakery, a family-owned business, that sells the best bread in town. And there's a branch of her credit union. The photography store always has the kind of film she prefers. The health food stores carries eggs from free-range chickens, which are difficult to find, especially in the winter months.

She thinks about the shopping centre's attitude toward the association for the mentally challenged as she walks into the health food store, even though it is spring and thoughts of Christmas should be the last thing on her mind. She has a Christmasy feeling within her, that same excitement and anticipation. The dinner party will be an evening of merriment. Good food, good music, stimulating conversation with friends.

The price of pistachios at the health food store astonishes her and brings her back to the present. But she pays the clerk without comment and drops the paper bag into her large shoulder bag, thinking it was just as well that she didn't buy the roses.

In the grocery store, she asks the young fellow who is piling oranges on a nearby counter if the grapes are from California. He doesn't know where the grapes are from and has to go to the back of the store, disappearing beyond a swinging door for a few minutes. She waits impatiently. It shouldn't matter, because Miriam said the boycott of Californian grapes has been off for a few years. "Just avoid anything from South Africa," Miriam had said. Does South Africa export grapes? She never thought to ask Miriam.

When the young fellow returns, he says, "They're from Chile," and then returns to the oranges. His lack of interest annoys her. Is this the sort of question he gets every day? Is he so lacking in curiosity? She wonders how he would look in a white satin evening gown and almost laughs as she fills a plastic bag with shiny, plump, purple grapes.

While she is paying for the grapes, it occurs to her that perhaps products from Chile are being boycotted because of all the human rights violations. But surely Miriam would have warned her. She puts the grapes in her shoulder bag and decides that if anyone at the dinner party asks where the grapes are from, she'll say she doesn't know.

After the grocery store, she goes to the bookstore and buys the latest book by Jane Rule. She wants something to read tomorrow, something to hold her attention and help her to relax. After a day like today, and the dinner party tonight, she will need to rest tomorrow. There's nothing on t.v. Sunday afternoons, so she will read. Does she have any white candles for the dinner table? She forgot to check. She decides to buy some at Woolworth's, in case there aren't any at home.

She returns to the apartment a few hours later, tired from fighting the Saturday crowds at the shopping mall, tired from lining up in every store, tired from carrying her increasingly heavy purchases from overheated store to store. She pauses outside the door, wondering what she will find inside.

She decides to knock once before unlocking the door and entering. She feels silly, knocking at her own door. The sharp smell of Mr. Clean greets her as she sets the pot of tulips on the library table. The flowers look perfect. The plastic bag is gone.

Clive walks into the living room. "Hello. You look tired. Want some coffee?"

Tired? What a rude thing to say. Glenda nods, speechless. He's...he's wearing an apron, a faded floral apron over a gaudy housedress of mauve and yellow pansies. And white ankle socks and grubby red knitted slippers, with a scarf on his head, a cotton scarf that's tied at the back of his neck. Everything about him looks old and tired. Except his eyes. He looks like a housewife. But a housewife from thirty or forty years ago. Isn't that how housewives looked back then? A modern housewife would never dress like that. She'd wear jeans and a t-shirt, or old polyester pants. Not a housedress of mauve and yellow pansies!

Does he realize his appearance leaves her wordless, her mind stuttering at the image of him? Even when he leaves the room, moving soundlessly in the knitted slippers, she still sees him standing there, a housewife, an aging cleaning lady, a...What is he? Not a lady. He's a man. A man can't be a lady. She is aware of the weight of the bag, hanging from her shoulder. How he dresses is none of her business. She removes her running shoes, leaving them in the tidy hall closet, and carries her shoulder bag into the kitchen. None of her business.

Clive is pouring coffee into a mug, his back to her. He looks like a weary...weary what? Why does he dress like *that* ?

"Where did you get that dress?"

"At the Salvation Army. I looked for weeks before I found it. Isn't it a great little frock. Do you take milk? Or sugar?"

"No. Black. Nothing in it. Black."

She is dying to ask more. Does anyone wear an apron anymore? The dress beneath the apron is worn and ancient looking. Would any woman be caught dead in it?

Clive hands her the mug and sits across from

her at the kitchen table, sipping from his own mug. It is very peculiar, she thinks, to be sitting across from a man wearing a dress. She knows it would not feel peculiar to sit across from a woman wearing a dress. That thought bothers her. But still, to sit across from anyone, man or woman, dressed in *that* dress.

"I'm almost finished. I did the kitchen first, so you can prepare for your soirée while I finish the rest of the place."

"Okay. I think I'll get started and drink my coffee while I work. I have a lot to do. I'll make lunch in a while. Would you like a salami sandwich?"

"That sounds good. I'm beginning to get hungry."

After he leaves, after she closes the kitchen door to give herself some privacy, she empties the red pistachios into a bright green ceramic bowl. She stands at the counter, admiring the contrasting colours of red against green. Why does the sight of him make her so uncomfortable?

Miriam arrives at six, an hour before the others are due, as they had arranged. She opens a bottle of white wine and pours some into two crystal goblets, while Glenda places white candles on the table and then puts the Camembert on the kitchen counter to soften and become creamy. Glenda joins Miriam at the table and leans forward, resting her arms on the linen tablecloth.

"Everything's ready. I haven't stopped all day."

"Your place looks cleaner than I've ever seen it. He did a good job."

Glenda nods and reaches for her goblet. "He's not coming back."

"Why not?"

"I told him I couldn't afford him on a regular

basis. That's almost true. I think I'll look for a woman to come in every two weeks. Would yours be interested?"

"I'll ask her if you want me to. She's pretty busy. She's very good, fast and efficient, so she can pick and choose her clients. Why won't you have him do it? Does he charge too much?"

"I don't know what the going rate is. He charges fourteen dollars an hour."

"Mine charges ten."

"Miriam, he dresses like a woman. I don't mean like a woman. Like a *wife*. He wears a housedress and an apron and hand-knitted slippers. How he dresses is none of my business. I know that." Glenda giggles and takes a long drink of wine. "He wears red knitted slippers. Don't say anything to anyone about him." She sat back in the chair. "Did you see the yellow tulips on the table in the living room? Aren't they perfect? Do you remember the day we went to the flea market and found that table? Do you remember lending me twenty dollars so I could buy it?"

The Heavens Cried

I wish I was one of those women who remember
all the details, who can recite every word of a
conversation years afterwards. I would write, "It
was five years ago but I remember it as if it was
yesterday. The sky was blue that day, a warm blue
with wisps of white clouds. Her house looked older
than it was, because green paint was peeling from
the front porch and the screen over the kitchen
window had two long ugly tears. The concrete
sidewalk leading up to the front door was broken
in many places, and bits of grass and scruffy
weeds grew in the cracks."

I don't know if any of that is true. I never drive
along her street anymore, never drive past the
house. Or that bus stop. I have to rely on memory.
The truth is, all I really remember is my feeling of
sadness. I remember the grief as if it was
yesterday.

Usually I try to forget. I prefer not to think
about it. I don't like feeling sad.

Darla's house. She was never concerned with
appearances. She lived alone there, except for a
tri-coloured cat and rooms of various green and
flowering plants. She always said she liked living
alone. I never quite believed her. Why would
anyone want to live alone?

Sometimes Darla said she preferred to live alone so she could write. She was a poet. Her mother and I published some of her poems last year in a small book with her name on the cover in solid green letters. Green was her favourite colour.

Other times, Darla said she lived alone because she needed solitude to keep her in touch with her feelings. She had an explanation for everything, sometimes numerous explanations for the same thing.

I wonder if she knew that some things defy explanation. I have never been able to explain her death. I've tried, Lord knows I've tried. That was almost my first thought, I remember that much, when I heard she was dead. Dead? Not Darla! Why? Why her? It didn't make sense. It defied logical reasoning. She was young, only thirty-nine, and healthy, although she smoked a pack a day and had done for twenty-odd years.

Somehow Darla's cat knew she was dead. The cat refused to eat and never ate again and died a week later, poor thing. I can understand that death, the cat not wanting to live without Darla.

I understand why people turn to religion when someone dies. Or to the occult, to seances. I understand the need to keep in touch, to feel able to communicate with the departed person. I have that need. I want to believe she exists, somewhere. I want to reach her.

I talk to her. Without religion or mediums. I talk to her in my mind. The day I slipped on ice and spent hours on a stretcher in Emergency, I told her she was right, I shouldn't wear heels, especially in winter. Was she shaking her head at me, the way she used to?

I was upset and angry with myself, lying there, wondering if my ankle was broken and how I would manage the stairs at work with a cast and crutches. The pain brought tears to my eyes. When the intern examined my leg and foot, I said, "My friend Darla always told me to wear flat boots in winter. I can hear her saying, 'I told you so.'"

He handed me a tissue and said, "You're going to be here for a while. We need x-rays. Do you want someone to phone her for you?"

It struck me as funny, his thinking he could phone her. I laughed. "Darla's dead. She was killed a few years ago."

He gave me the strangest look.

Yes Darla, I know, but I was frightened, and my ankle hurt so much. I didn't think before I spoke. Were you frightened? Did you feel pain? Was there time? Did it happen in slow motion? Or was it so fast it was all over before you knew it?

My ankle wasn't broken, just a cracked bone. They wrapped it and told me to stay off it for a few days, apply ice for the swelling, and take 222's for the pain. Before they let me go, a psychiatrist came to my cubicle.

She said, "The doctor tells me someone close to you passed away recently."

"Not recently. Five years ago." I hate it when people say "passed away."

"Did you have some counselling at the time?"

"No."

"Would you like to talk about it now?"

"No."

She gave me her business card and left. I guess I spooked that intern. But why didn't *he* ask me about it? He didn't say a word to me, just summoned a psychiatrist? Coward.

I threw her business card away when I got home. What does it matter. What is there to say? There is no explanation. No one's been able to give me one. I don't accept the idea that it was God's will. If there is a God, which I doubt, why would this God take Darla?

And the sadness, it isn't so bad anymore. Just every once in a long while, when I haven't talked to her for weeks, I feel like crying. I do cry, sometimes. Afterwards, I always talk to her. Darla, I say, Can you hear me? I hope so. Do you know I am thinking of you? Do you feel these tears with me?

Sometimes I try to reconstruct that morning and I imagine how the last day of her life began. I lived with her once, years ago, when we were younger. That was before she insisted on living alone. Even then, she liked a lot of solitude. Used to spend hours in her room with the door closed. I knew many of her habits. And I have pictures of her. I wish I had taken more.

She'd wake up in the morning to the alarm buzzing. She owned the most bizarre clock-radio I've ever seen. Her father bought it in France on one of his business trips. It looked like a cat. The cat's open mouth held a radio instead of teeth. The left eye was the face of a clock. It was one of those things that's so ugly it's almost beautiful.

Darla loved it. She set it so the alarm went off at six, then the radio clicked on and played music for ten minutes. She liked to wake up to music. She said it eased the transition from sleeping to waking.

She took a shower as soon as she got out of bed. She washed her hair every day and then would stand naked, in front of the mirror, blow-drying it. She liked her body, although she once told me her shoulders were too broad. She liked to walk around the house with nothing on. Even when we lived together.

She'd have her first cigarette as she got dressed. There was always an ashtray in her bedroom, but she never smoked in bed. She said that was asking for trouble.

But really, who can predict what will bring trouble? Darla was a careful pedestrian. She said cars were lethal weapons, as dangerous as guns. The lessons of childhood, look both ways twice before crossing the street, always wait until the light turns green, don't step out between parked cars, did not spare her even though she had learned them well. How did it happen? The police told her parents that the driver lost control of his car. How else could they explain a car driving over a sidewalk and striking a bench, a bus stop sign, and Darla? By the time it got to court, they were saying he fell asleep at the wheel.

My precious Darla. Did she see it coming? Did she have time to be scared, time to know she was close to death? Did she see the driver, see his eyes as the car struck her?

It doesn't matter. It's long over. She's gone.

Once she was dressed, she would eat breakfast. Toast or a muffin and coffee. She adored coffee. She liked the strong kind made from black beans. I remember she once said the smell of freshly ground beans was the most delicious smell in the world, and the taste of the coffee was never quite as exciting. She worried about caffeine, just as she worried about the cigarettes, but her love for them, her addictions, clouded her judgement.

In the end it didn't matter. Trouble didn't come from the caffeine or the cigarettes. Trouble came from a driver who lost control of his car.

She walked out of her house, the house that desperately needed painting, and walked to the bus stop, to get a bus to work. Was it a good morning for her? Or was she worried because her mortgage was coming up for renewal, and she had used the last can of cat food but didn't have time to get to the grocery store which sold that brand? Her cat was finicky and would only eat the one particular kind.

Did you know, Darla, that your mother drove all over the city hunting for the right kind of cat food, even though she cried all day and that night. Her grief was so great that she couldn't smile for months. It's sort of funny, when you think about it. Your mother's desperate search for cat food didn't matter either. It was all for nothing. The cat refused to eat, even sardines and cheddar cheese which were her favourite treats.

I miss you. I'll never have another friend like you.

Sometimes I read your poems. That one about the washing machine always makes me laugh. You had a great sense of humour. I never told you, when you were alive. I regret that. I regret... I forget and I don't want to. Sometimes I can't remember what you look like and I have to get out the pictures. I wish I had taken more.

Were you looking the other way, thinking about a poem perhaps? Or enjoying the clear blue sky? Was it a clear blue sky? I can't remember. I do remember that it rained the day of your funeral. How appropriate. That's what I thought at the time. Now, on certain rainy days, when the trees are bare and the rain falls endlessly, I am sad and I think about you.

I'd never been to court before. The trial wasn't anything like they are on television.

The driver was charged with reckless driving. He pleaded not guilty. He was a doctor, suffering from stress and exhaustion. It was from caring for sick people, his colleagues testified. He often saw seventy or more patients a day. It was not his fault, they insisted. He fell asleep at the wheel because he was tired and overworked. His patients loved him. He was a good man, respected in the community. It wasn't his fault. Darla's death was just an unfortunate accident.

The trial was a farce. I felt so helpless. They didn't care that you were dead. From what I could see, everyone wanted to save the doctor's career. Even the Crown Attorney, who was supposed to be prosecuting the murderer. The doctor received a suspended sentence. I bet he's still seeing seventy patients a day, making more money than he has time to spend, all in the name of helping people. How much help is he when each person gets six or seven minutes of his time?

It still makes me angry. I try not to think about him, but to concentrate on Darla.

I remember the time we went to Montreal just for the hell of it. We were bored. It was Darla's idea, to take the bus and wander around Montreal for the day. The best part was supper at an outdoor café on a street lined with restaurants. We shared a bottle of wine and talked for hours. Darla talked about her new job with the AIDS Committee. She cared about people, really cared, always did. She said the openness and courage of the men living with AIDS made her feel humble. They lived in the moment, expressed their feelings, spoke their thoughts. She said other things about her new job, but I forget what she said.

Then we talked about our mothers. Mine, who spent most of my life in and out of psychiatric hospitals. Darla was always fond of Mother, but, she confided in me that evening as we watched the sun set behind the city buildings, she had always been a little afraid of her. Not afraid for her own sake, because she knew my mother only tried to harm herself. Afraid for my sake.

She didn't smile at me across the small round table. Afraid that I would learn the craziness, she said.

I remember watching the smoke from her cigarette and thinking we are all a little crazy in our own way. I smiled. She asked, Why are you smiling?

I said I knew she didn't mean I might inherit my mother's mental illness, that desperate despair that haunted my mother every day of her life. Darla is an educated woman. I mean, she was. She knew emotional sickness is not inherited, like the colour of my eyes or the shape of my breasts, but that it can be learned. Yet for some reason she never understood that I have learned, instead, how to be always logical and reasonable. I have also learned how to forget certain things. I had tried to explain it to her a few times over the years, but she never understood.

Then we talked of her mother. I can almost see Darla in my mind, sipping wine and holding a

cigarette in her right hand, describing her
mother's sixtieth birthday party.

I never told you that sometimes I resented
your relationship with your mother. It was more
like a friendship than a mother-daughter
relationship. I considered telling you that evening
in Montreal, that I was jealous of the way you
were with your mother. I remember that much.
But I didn't want to spoil the closeness between
us. Did you know I envied you?

I still see Darla's mother. We meet for brunch
every few months, on a Sunday. We always talk
about Darla, but mostly we talk about what we're
doing in our lives.

I'll never forget the bus trip back. We giggled
all the way home like schoolgirls, and held hands
as if we were lovers. I suppose we were lovers,
always had been, except for the sex part. Darla, I
miss you.

It's been raining all day. I wish I could
remember every word of our conversation at that
outdoor café. How was I to know you would be
dead a month later. What does it mean to be
dead? Darla, are you sitting here with me right
now? When I close my eyes, you are.

Red, Red Leaves

Emily stared at the small package in her left hand, thinking it looked like a compact cake of soft cinnamon. She stood alone in the dimly-lit health food store, alone except for the clerk, peering at the package and trying to make a decision.

As she debated, she was aware of the woman waiting patiently on the other side of the counter. Or was the clerk waiting impatiently? Why did she stand there like that, silent and stern. Did she think Emily would drop the package in her bag and run out the door without paying for it?

Should I buy it? Make up your mind, she told herself. And don't take all day about it. She squeezed the package gently and the powdery mass shifted slightly, like tiny grains of sand but softer. She turned the package over and read the label. *Red Egyptien Henna $1.49 100 g.*

It's cheap, only a dollar forty-nine. What can I lose? Even if I don't use it, it's not a lot of money. I can afford it. *Red Egyptien Henna.* Should I? Make a decision. Just make a decision.

"I'll take it," Emily said, looking up as she spoke to smile at the woman.

The woman did not smile in return. She reached for the small package. "Do you want a bag?"

"Yes. Please. To protect it."

Emily left the store quickly, not pausing to put the change from the two-dollar bill into her change purse. She slipped the coins into the pocket of her jeans, and carried the small paper bag in her hand.

At home, a fifteen-minute bus ride later, she stood at the kitchen window looking at the maple tree for a few minutes, before allowing herself the pleasure of opening the paper bag. The tree was on a neighbour's property, but some of the long branches stretched over her backyard. That corner of the yard was hidden beneath brown and yellow leaves. Most of the leaves had fallen and the upper half of the tree was completely bare. The branches trembled and waved in the wind. Every so often, yellowing leaves fluttered downward. The remaining leaves, the fiery orange ones and the brilliant red ones, would fall within the next few days. The days were getting wintry and the dark evenings brought bone-chilling cold.

Emily shivered. She closed the window, opened the bag and pulled out the cellophane package. Near the window, in natural light, the cake of fine powder looked green, with tiny flecks of yellow. She read the label again. *Red Egyptien Henna.* Surely *Egyptien* is spelled wrong, she thought. It's spelled as it would be in French. Not that that's wrong.

Feeling safe in the privacy of her own kitchen, she did what she had not dared to do under the impatient glare of the clerk. She rested the small cellophane package against the side of her nose and sniffed. She sniffed again, a slow deep breath, and then another two sniffs, shallow and rapid. No scent. Nothing. If the powder had a smell, the cellophane kept it secret.

Emily placed the package on the counter, beside a bowl of Empire apples, and moved to the other counter. She stood before the untidy stacks of dirty dishes, glasses, flatware, pots, and lids, and rolled up her sleeves.

As she rinsed suds from a plate, she glanced at the small package. It seemed too outrageous, this idea of turning her hair red. What had possessed her? If she looked like a different woman, a red-headed woman, would the clerk have been rude to her?

She was wiping puddles of soapy water from the counter when Willa arrived home. "You don't look happy." She squeezed excess water from the dish cloth.

"I'm tired. It was a long day."

"I bought some henna on my way home. Want to see it?" Emily folded the dish cloth and draped it over the edge of the sink.

"You're going to dye your hair?"

"I've been thinking about it. It might be fun."

"What colour will it make your hair?"

"Red. Like those leaves out there."

Willa glanced at the tree and poked the cellophane package with her forefinger. "Do you know what to do with it?"

"Sure. I read the instructions on the bulletin board at the health food store. It's a simple process and very easy."

"It's funny-looking stuff." Willa poured herself a glass of skim milk and closed the fridge door. "I don't know why you want to bother." She emptied the glass in two long swallows.

The package of henna sat on the kitchen counter for two weeks. Emily was busy, too busy to use it, always rushing here and there. She thought about using it whenever she noticed the small cellophane package on the counter. But I

don't have time right now, she kept telling herself.
I'll try it as soon as I have time.

Other times she told herself, I am who I am and
it's foolish to want to be different.

Willa did not mention the small package.

It suited Emily to be occupied with other things.
She was afraid to use the henna. The impulse to
buy it came from some need within her for drastic
change, a wish to look totally different. These
feelings alarmed her. She hoped they would go
away. If she ignored her feelings for a few weeks,
they always passed. Except she could rarely
ignore her feelings for very long.

Emily was beginning to recognize a pattern in
her life. When the seasons changed, she felt a
need to transform herself into someone different.
The extreme changes which signaled radical shifts
in temperature, winter to spring and then fall to
winter, meant reorganizing her wardrobe. It
happened over a period of weeks. In September
and October, light-weight cotton and short sleeves
were exchanged for long sleeves and heavy
sweaters. Bright colours were carefully folded and
put away, in a large cardboard box at the back of
her closet, to be replaced by drab, dark colours.
She went through the opposite process during
April and May.

Twice a year, during October and May, she
would haunt the clothing stores downtown,
looking for new clothes and a new image. She
longed for a new look. But who did she want to
look like?

She disliked shopping for clothes. Wandering
from store to store, looking at this, trying on that,
she ended up tired and close to exhaustion. As
soon as she entered a store she tried to avoid the

salesperson. It was always women selling in
women's clothing stores.

Did she need or want a new pair of trousers?
That black pair? What did she have at home that
would match them? Her mind was a blank as she
tried to envision the interior of her closet, as if the
closet was empty. It didn't matter. Black goes with
everything. Emily would lift the trousers off the
rack, to take a closer look. Was $49.99 (And why,
she wondered, aren't they priced $49.31 or
$50.09?) too much for this particular pair of
trousers? Did the quality of the cotton, the
stitching, justify paying fifty dollars plus eight
percent tax for these black trousers?

Then there was the changing room. A small
cubicle with perhaps one hook or, with luck, one
small stool to hold her clothes while she tried on
the black trousers. Usually there was a mirror in
the cubicle, so she could evaluate herself in
private. She felt an obligation to decide quickly,
not to occupy the cubicle too long. If she turned
this way and that, undecided, she would tell
herself not to buy the trousers. Indecision was a
bad sign. The ideal situation was to love the
garment at first glance. That felt safer, surer.

Did they fit? Did they suit her? Was the waist
too loose? The derrière too snug? Would she like
them next week? Next month?

Trudging from store to store, the possibility of
returning home empty-handed loomed large in her
mind. She felt like a failure, all those wasted
hours, if she went home with nothing. How
complicated can shopping be? Others seemed to
do it with ease. Shopping was not fun, not
pleasure, was rarely satisfying. And when she
found a new garment, even if it was something she

adored at first sight, she didn't become a different woman, never turned into a beautiful and sexy woman, an elegant woman, a saucy and fun woman. Never ever did she turn into a wildly exciting androgynous creature, someone who was defined by her spirit and energy, rather than her clothes and sex.

She hated shopping for shoes more than anything. Finding comfortable flat shoes was a feat surpassed only by getting a good haircut. She drifted into the more expensive shoe stores, believing pricey shoes were better-fitting and longer-lasting, discouraged before she has scanned the samples on display. The salespeople in these stores were as likely to be men as women.

There were no words to describe her sense of accomplishment when, on that rare occasion, she found a pair of ultra-comfortable walking shoes.

She never seemed able to turn herself into the new woman. She remained Emily. As the temperature stabilized and she adjusted to the new season, she wore the same old clothes, with a couple of recent additions that rarely matched the old favourites, and settled back into the routines of her life.

She wasn't sure when it started, this pattern of wanting to transform herself twice a year. But she had learned to count on it. The urges to revamp herself came every six months, as surely as the leaves fell from the trees each October and rain and tulips came each May.

Willa didn't seem to suffer from this seasonal compulsion. She went shopping midway through the season, when everything was on sale. She only shopped when she absolutely had to replace an aging article from her wardrobe, and she always bought clothes on sale. Willa was immune to Emily's feverish compulsion. How, Emily wondered, just how had Willa escaped?

Emily stood in the bathroom, brushing her hair and studying herself in the full-length mirror on the back of the door. This fall, she wanted to change the colour of her hair. She wondered where this yearning came from, and why now? Wanting new clothes was one thing. That was an established part of the pattern. But changing the colour of her hair? It was a crazy idea. How could she even consider it?

She knew a few women who coloured their hair. Some did it to hide the grey hairs and tried to match the colour of their other hairs. One friend, Martha, used coloured styling gel on her hair, and it turned the white hairs a brassy orange. The bright orange stood out among all the light brown hair. It suited her friend, but Emily couldn't imagine looking like that. She wanted something less obvious, more subtle, less drastic, more... what?

Another friend did it once, dyed her hair, turning dark brown hair to blonde because blondes had more fun. She wanted more fun in her life, Nicole said. A few months later she had confided to Emily that she didn't enjoy being a blonde. She'd never do it again. People treated her differently. People didn't treat her like a fun-loving woman. They treated her more like a helpless and vaguely stupid woman. Nicole was straight. Emily understood that when her blonde-haired friend said *people*, she meant *men*.

Sue, a woman at work, got a perm last year. She said she had envied people with naturally curly hair all her life. But afterwards she didn't

like it, didn't like the way her hair kinked and
stuck out all over. Emily thought the curly hair
suited her. Perhaps Sue didn't believe her,
perhaps she didn't care for Emily's opinion
although she had asked for it. Sue moaned for
months, until she finally had her hair cut short
just to get rid of the perm.

Emily wondered why she wanted to change the
colour of her hair. She surely didn't want to
become a blonde, had never wanted to be a blonde
woman. Just as she had never wanted curly hair
or large breasts. She had never aspired to be
Marilyn Monroe. She liked her body, liked the size
and shape of her breasts, liked her dark hair and
the few freckles across her nose. She wanted to
change herself in other ways, to dress elegantly or
fashionably. But she couldn't understand where
this new urge came from, this wanting to dye her
hair.

She wished her hair would start turning white
and grey. She had an image of herself as she
would be one day, a mature woman, a respected
and wise woman with shoulder-length hair, an
attractive blend of white and grey, with grey hair
curling out around her ears like wings. She would
wear a massive silver bracelet on her right wrist
and black trousers and silky long white shirts.
When she became this mature woman, she would
let her short hair grow and flow around her face.
For now, her hair was short.

Each morning she reached for an apple from
the bowl, to eat as she walked to work. She
resisted the urge to touch the package of henna.
Instead, she looked out the window at the tree and
tried to talk herself into using the henna, daring
herself to take a risk. The tree was bare. The

ground was hidden beneath a lumpy patchwork quilt of scarlet, mustard, pumpkin, and earthy brown leaves. "Henna is good for your hair," she said to Willa one evening, as she washed the dishes. "Some women use it to condition their hair."

Willa was chopping onions for carrot soup. "Do we have any celery?"

"Yes. We got some when we were shopping on Saturday. Henna's a vegetable compound. No chemicals, no crap."

"When are you going to do it?"

Emily frowned as she scrubbed at hard flecks of porridge inside a small aluminum pot. Now that the mornings were cool and crisp they ate porridge for breakfast, rather than cold cereals from the health food store. "I'll need your help. How about tomorrow night?"

"Fine. We'll have to do it right after supper. I'm going to that poetry reading at nine."

"Wil, what if my hair turns green? Like Anne of Green Gables." Could it turn green, she wondered. Was henna an unstable substance?

"You'll stand out in a crowd." Willa turned to look at Emily and laughed. "Green hair might suit you."

It had been a serious question, a real fear. But, Emily assured herself, my hair won't turn green. That would never happen to me. Those kinds of things only happen in books.

The following evening, after supper, they spread everything they would need along the kitchen counter: the package of henna, a glass bowl, an old soup spoon which didn't match their cutlery, two worn-out bath towels, a box of Saran Wrap, and a roll of paper towels.

They had talked during supper about applying the henna and tried to anticipate each step of the procedure and the tools required. It was fun, like preparing for an adventure together. They giggled as they leaned toward one another across the table. While Emily stood in the shower, washing her hair, Willa dumped the package of henna into the glass bowl and added hot, hot water from the tap, stirring the mixture into a thick, dark-brown paste.

Emily walked into the kitchen wearing old shabby clothes, her wet hair combed neatly. "It smells like a stable in here."

"This stuff stinks, all right. And it looks like mud. Look at it." Willa held the bowl out to Emily and wrinkled her nose. "Doesn't it look awful."

"Do you think we should do this?"

"Sit down. Let's get it over with." Willa kissed Emily's damp forehead. "Are you ready?"

Emily nodded and sat on an old wooden stool in the centre of the kitchen, the floor around her covered with newspaper. Willa held the bowl in the crook of her arm and used her other hand to plaster the earthy-smelling paste all over Emily's short hair. As she worked, Willa chatted about an article she had read on censorship. It was a topical issue receiving a great deal of attention in the feminist press.

Emily was interested in the issue of censorship, but she barely heard Willa as she thought about *Red Egyptien* and wondered what colour her hair would be in a few hours. Will my hair turn some awful colour? she wondered. No, it couldn't. Will I like it? Which shade of red will it turn? She had meant to look up *Egyptien* in the dictionary, to see if that was the French spelling. It had an exotic air to it, *Red Egyptien*.

The runny paste cooled quickly against Emily's scalp and the coldness made her shiver. Clumps of moist henna fell to the floor, staining the newspapers with greenish-brown spots. Emily stared at the scattered stains. This stuff stinks, she thought. Will my hair turn the colour of those spots? Will I smell like this for days? She remembered using diluted vinegar as a creme rinse when she was in her teens. On the days when it rained and her hair got wet as she walked to school, she lived with a faint vinegary odour.

Willa talked as she worked, about the need for, no, not the need for but the right to freedom of expression. She encased the hennaed hair in long pieces of Saran Wrap, wrapping the transparent strips around and around. There had to be another way to deal with pornography, a way that did not give government the power to suppress real art. She covered the plastic layers with an old towel to form a huge bulky turban on Emily's head.

Willa washed her hands three times, first with soap and water, then with Comet, then with soap and water again, but she could not wash away the orangey-brown stains on her fingernails. They laughed about this.

Emily wondered, Will my hair turn that orangey-brown colour? She wanted a deep red colour. She could see herself sitting at her desk in her office with a cap of rich dark-red hair. Orangey-brown did not fit the image she had in mind.

Emily sat on the stool, surrounded by newspapers speckled with drops of drying green-brown henna, and read a paperback. She tried not to think about the colour of her hair, tried not to

think about the weight on her head, tried instead
to concentrate on the novel, *The Sophie Horowitz
Story* by Sarah Schulman.

She wanted to stop after half an hour. Her back
was aching from sitting on the uncomfortable
stool and her shoulders were sore from the cold
weight on her head.

"I'm freezing," she called out, closing the
paperback abruptly.

Willa came from the living room and stood
before Emily with her hands on her hips.

"What's the problem?"

"I'm tired. I don't think this is a good idea."

"It can't do any harm. That's what you said."

"I'm bored."

"We'll do it differently next time, okay? I won't
put so much water in the henna, so it doesn't leak
like this. Then you can sit anywhere. You can
watch t.v. while it takes."

She made Emily a cup of tea, peppermint with a
drop of honey, and urged her to be calm and wait
a little longer. "Be patient and drink the tea while
it's still hot. It'll be over soon."

Emily took the tea and held the glass mug with
both hands, trying to warm herself.

Willa picked up the novel from her lap. "Is this
any good?"

"I think so. I can't get into it. I'm too
uncomfortable!"

They waited another thirty minutes, precisely
timed by the kitchen clock. Willa washed the
muddy henna from Emily's hair, with Emily bent
over the sink, her shoulders protected by an old
bath towel. Emily thought about her image of
herself as a mature woman, with white and grey
hairs, as Willa made a lather with shampoo and

massaged her scalp. When would her hair start to change colour naturally?

"Be careful! You're getting shampoo in my eyes."

"Hold still. I'm almost done."

"What colour it is? Can you see any difference?"

"No, I can't." Willa rinsed away the shampoo with cupfuls of warm water. "Your hair feels soft, though. Very soft. Maybe we didn't leave it on long enough. I'm almost finished here, then you can see for yourself in the mirror. It doesn't seem to have done anything. But it may look different as it dries. The colour could show more then."

Emily liked the feel of Willa's hands massaging her head. She wanted it to go on forever, the soothing hands then the warming shower of hot water. Was this all a waste of time? Had the *Red Egyptien Henna* left her exactly as she was before? Questions, questions, she thought, grinding her teeth. I'm sick of all these questions. I can't ever seem to make up my mind. What do I want?

"You're done," Willa said, wrapping a dry towel around Emily's wet hair. "I'm going to get ready to go to the poetry reading. If Martha phones, tell her I'm leaving now."

"Okay. Thanks for helping. I'm going to look in the mirror and see what it's like."

I'll try again if it didn't take this time, she decided as she peered at herself in the full-length mirror. She used her fingers to comb through the wet hair, searching for a hint of red. Why didn't it work? Next time I'll try a different kind of henna. From a different health store.

Cold Climates

I can't think about anything else. I keep trying.
Sometimes it works for a few minutes, like when I
skimmed through the newspaper before lunch.
But as soon as I reached for my cup of tea, I
remembered and my stomach heaved and I started
crying all over again. Sitting here by the window,
looking out at the snow, everything is a blur.

You never know how much someone means to
you until you think you might lose them. I mean,
you just take people for granted. And now it may
be too late. Please don't let it be too late.

I've been sitting here since before lunch and it's
been snowing the whole time, a gentle snow that
falls and falls. From the window it looks like a
winter scene from a Hollywood movie, one of those
romantic black and white 1940's movies. It's the
perfect kind of snowfall for Christmas–large, soft
flakes and everything's covered with a layer of
clean white snow.

I hate my tears and I hate waiting. I hate the
snow and I hate December. I hate December more
than July when it's so hot I can barely breathe.
This part of the country's got the worst weather.
It's unbearably cold outside in winter but it's like
an oven indoors because everyone overheats their

homes and offices. In summer the humid heat is suffocating and everyone uses air conditioning to make it like a freezer indoors.

It's got to be the worst month of the twelve. What with the weather and Christmas, December is the month of stress. The weather's been getting colder for weeks and the shock hit me around the second day of December. Winter is here, no question about it, and it's not going to be warm again for months and months. Not unless you're one of those that can afford to go to Florida for a few weeks in January, to get away from it all.

I wish I could get away from it all.

My Aunt Susan did that last year, went south in January to get away from the subzero temperatures and blowing snow. She's not one of those that can afford holidays. But two years ago she won a lottery. Well! She thought she was independently wealthy.

The first thing Aunt Susan did was open a savings account. She'd never had one before. But she's no fool, my Aunt Susan. She said she was putting the five thousand dollars into a savings account, so she would make some interest on her money while she figured out what to do with it.

You know what she did? She bought me a Canada Savings Bond, worth five hundred dollars, for Christmas that year. I thought *I* was independently wealthy. I still have it. It's my 'in case' money. In case I lose my job or something and need money. I'm tempted to cash it in right now and use the money to go to Florida. Is five hundred dollars enough to go to Florida?

But I can't leave. I have to sit here and wait.

After she opened the savings account and bought me the Canada Savings Bond, Aunt Susan bought herself a winter coat. It's a fine wool one in a pretty shade of blue with green trim. Then she bought gloves, a hat, a scarf, and boots, all in the same shade of blue to match the coat. She shopped for a whole day to find everything, but it was worth it. She looked warm and smart, and I could tell she felt special every time she got dressed to go out.

She didn't buy anything else for a couple of months. She said she needed some time to think carefully, so she wouldn't do something rash. She had $26.71 in interest at the end of the first month. She showed me her savings book. She was awfully proud of that interest.

A month later she said she'd been thinking about it and it felt immoral to make money on the money in her bank account without doing anything to actually earn the interest. She said she was awfully disappointed in herself. She had actually been thrilled when interest rates went up because it meant she'd make more money. And then she remembered there were people who had to borrow money to live and had to pay even more interest to do it. She said she was compromising her principles and she'd better spend the money so she couldn't earn more interest. Either that or take it out of the bank and keep it under her pillow, where it couldn't make a penny of interest.

I was with her the day she went to the bank to close the savings account. When the teller asked why she was closing her account and Aunt Susan told her, the teller looked up from her official form and stared. She said, "I've never heard that reason before." She put her pen down and asked if she could shake Aunt Susan's hand. After they shook, she told Aunt Susan that she could open a

chequing account which did not earn interest. So
Aunt Susan did that and felt better immediately.

In April she bought a VCR, new living room
curtains, and a little freezer that sits in her
bedroom beside the closet door.

She was so excited about the freezer. The next
time I went to see her, she dragged me into her
bedroom to admire it. What's there to say about a
freezer? It's an appliance. I tried to think of something to say, because it meant so much to her.

Every time she cooks a meal, she makes
enough to freeze some for later. She stores the
meals in margarine containers; each one has a
little white label that tell you what's in there and
when she cooked it. She says it fills her with joy to
open the door and see rows of ready-to-heat
nutritious food.

All fall she talked of using the money that was
left to buy herself a used car. She's always wanted
a car. Especially in winter. She gets cold, standing
at bus stops. I know what she means. Sometimes I
think I'll turn into an icicle before the bus arrives.
The bus will come and there I'll be, frozen solid to
the ground, unable to move, a gigantic icicle. But
she didn't buy a car. She liked having a little
money sitting safely in the bank. She called it her
nest egg.

She gave up all thought of the used car when
she saw the poster. It was a bitterly cold
December day. We'd been downtown together,
Christmas shopping. Aunt Susan looked so good
in her blue coat and matching hat and gloves and
boots. We were trudging our way through the
snow to have lunch at the cafeteria around the
corner from the library. The stores had been hot
and crowded, and we were tired.

The poster was on the window of a travel agency. It showed a tanned white woman, wearing a black bikini. She was smiling and standing on a sunny beach, her bare feet half-buried in the warm sand. The blue ocean and sunny sky stretched out forever behind her.

Aunt Susan stopped and stared. "Wouldn't it be nice to be there."

"Sure."

"Come on. Let's go inside and see what it costs. Just for the fun of it."

She paid for the trip, right there and then. She didn't even phone her boss to make sure she could have the time off work. The extreme cold had gone to her head. That, and winning the lottery money that made her independently wealthy.

She didn't go to Florida. Not my Aunt Susan. You see, she's a feminist and she's got all sorts of principles. Feminists! They're becoming as common as VCRs. Almost every family's got one.

And of all the warm, sunny places in the world–Florida, Bermuda, Brazil–she picked Cuba. It's because of her principles. She wouldn't consider Florida or any of those other sunny spots. The travel agent showed her a lovely brochure for a resort in Jamaica. I did my best to persuade her to go there. No luck. It had to be Cuba.

It has to be a socialist country, she said, and preferably one that advances the status of women. I didn't say anything because I was brought up to respect my elders. My Aunt Susan reads a lot and she's a self-educated woman but she doesn't know everything. I've read about Cuba in the newspaper and I can't believe such a repressive government does anything good for women. And I hear it's not worth your life to be a lesbian there.

Just between you and me, I'd take Cuba over this frosty cold and snow. But given the choice, I'd sooner take Florida or that resort in Jamaica. There wasn't even a brochure with glossy pictures for Cuba! Just a typed page of information. No style there. No class at all.

When Aunt Susan got home from Cuba, we had another one of our feminist fights. She sent me a postcard from Cuba, you see. For all the principles they have in Cuba, they have postcards for the tourists. I still have the postcard on my fridge. Every time I look at it, I think of principles. I can see it from here, if I turn my head. It's all blurred because of these damned tears.

She sent me this postcard and addressed it to *Ms* Elizabeth. That made me furious. And I told her so when she got back, right there at the airport. I don't believe in that Miz business. I'm a Miss and proud of it.

I said to her, as soon as I saw her tanned face, "Don't you ever call me Miz again. I'm a Miss and always will be."

She smiled. Now, that was unusual. Usually when we discuss this feminist stuff, she starts frowning and lecturing me before I have time to take a breath.

"It's nice to be home. I had a wonderful time, thank you," she said, smiling the whole time. "You're right, Elizabeth. The least I can do is respect how you wish to be addressed." She put her hand over mine. "But seriously, child, all men are called Mister. We don't try to identify them by their marital status. Why divide women into Mrs. and Miss? Why make it important to know if a woman is married or not?"

Well! She was lecturing me, which was normal,

but she was smiling, which was not. That trip must have relaxed her. But I hate it when she calls me child. Makes me feel like a child when I'm an adult.

"I don't care what men do. Or what they don't do, for that matter! It's silly nonsense like all that feminist stuff."

"Silly nonsense? Elizabeth. As a Miss, you're an object of pity in this world. Women are supposed to want to be married. Your goal in life is to be called Mrs. You call that silly nonsense?"

"I sure do. That's their problem, not mine. I'm a Miss and proud of it. I'm my own woman!"

Where had her fighting spirit gone? She was still smiling. "You keep on like this, and you won't get the present I brought you."

That shut me up. I'm not one to stick to silly principles for nothing. "You bought me something? What did you get? Where is it?"

"Get my suitcase for me, will you? It's the big brown one I borrowed from your mother. Your present's in there."

I got her suitcase and lugged it out to a taxi. The day was bitterly cold, you know the way it gets in January, and she was shivering in summer clothes under her blue wool coat. I could hear her teeth chattering beside me all the way home. As soon as we were inside her apartment, she opened the suitcase. Do you know what she brought me? A black shawl in a silky material with gigantic red flowers embroidered on it. I'm wearing it right now. It feels so nice to touch. Soft and smooth. I've never had anything like it before. It's special. And so is my Aunt Susan.

I talked to her on the phone this morning. She's in the hospital. A lump in her breast. They're operating this afternoon, to take a biopsy and see what it is. I can't visit her. I can't! I can't stand to see her in that hospital bed. The smell of the hospital makes my stomach heave. I phone her every day, sometimes three times a day. She says she'll be all right. She's just worried because she hasn't finished her Christmas shopping. She calls it Solstice shopping. I can't remember why she calls it that, although she has explained it to me. It is something to do with feminism, you can be sure.

She's read books so she can make an informed decision, and she's been fighting with the surgeon, who keeps telling her to trust him. But, as she says, she only met him three weeks ago and doesn't know him from Adam, so why on earth should she trust him? She said that to his face. She's got some nerve, my Aunt Susan.

She'd rather have a woman surgeon, but there isn't one in this city who specializes in breasts. I have to admit she makes sense. What can a man know about breasts? I sure don't know much about testicles. I've read about them and seen a few pictures, but it's not the same as actually having a pair.

The doctor was furious when she'd only sign a consent form for the biopsy. He wanted her to give him a blanket consent, to do what he likes, what he thinks best while she's under the anaesthetic, even if it means removing one or both breasts and muscles and lymph nodes and all sorts of things. Just thinking about it puts my stomach in knots.

He doesn't know my Aunt Susan. She's read everything she can get her hands on. I bet she knows as much as he does. It seems that surgery is not always the best approach. But, as she says, you can't expect a surgeon to agree. Cutting up bodies is his life's work. She said that to his face, too. She said she understood that removing parts of bodies was what he did for a living, and her own doctor said he was very good at it, and she understood that he had to believe in what he does, but her body was important to her and she had to do what she thought was best.

My Aunt Susan is a very understanding woman. You could never hope to meet anyone as understanding as she is. She tries to see and understand all points of view. It sounds like the surgeon was not so understanding. He said he'd never had a patient like her before. His patients *always* trust him. He'd been doing this for many years and he knew what was best for her.

Who did he think he was, talking to Aunt Susan like that! When she told me, I got so angry and agitated that I pulled the telephone cord out of the wall and cut her off and had to plug it back in and call her back.

She told him she trusted him, but when she was telling me about it she admitted that was a small lie. She felt she had to say it, though, because he was so very upset. She can't bear to lie but she felt she had to say something to calm him down. She offered to go downstairs to the cafeteria with him and have a nice cup of hot tea and discuss it some more, but he refused. He said he didn't have time. He was very busy and had many other patients to see, and besides that she wasn't supposed to leave the floor.

Under all that strength, I know she's scared. I should be there with her, helping her fight. But I don't know what to say or what to do. I keep crying, whenever I think about it. I just want her to be all right.

She says she will be. But how can she know for sure?

I hate Christmas. It's not the snow and cold. It's Christmas. The stores are packed with miserable people, who'd as soon cut your throat as smile at you. There's nothing merry about Christmas. Have you noticed? It's all misery. Damned expensive misery. My VISA bill in January is going to be a whopper. I hate Christmas. I HATE IT!

I feel awful, like I'm letting her down. But I don't know what to do or say. She wants to talk about the possibility that it's cancer and about being scared. It upsets me. I know it's disgusting, the way I'm feeling sorry for myself. But she has always been the one to look after me. Now she needs to be looked after and I don't know how. All I want to do is cry. If it stops snowing by supper time, I'll bundle up in all my warmest clothes and catch a bus and go in this evening to visit her. But I know she'll understand if I don't. I'll cry if I go in there. I can't cry in front of her. It will upset her.

She came to see me in hospital when I had my tonsils out. I was a scared kid, only thirteen. She brought me ice cream, chocolate, my favourite flavour, and a stuffed bear wearing sunglasses. I still have the bear. Her name's Inny and she sits on my bed.

Aunt Susan asked the nurse that's been looking after her to phone me as soon as they know the results of the biopsy. But the phone doesn't ring, it just sits there. Surely it's over by now, surely they know. I wish they'd phone. This waiting is driving me crazy.

When she phoned me at lunch time today, my lunch time not her lunch time, because they won't let her eat or drink anything before the operation,

she said no one wants to use the word cancer.
That's making her angry.

"When the doctor was in this morning, I asked
him what my chances were that it was cancer. He
said not to worry about it, everything will be all
right."

"Well, he must know what he's talking about."

"And my own doctor was in last night. When I
asked her if she thought it was cancer she said
not to make mountains out of molehills and that
she knows everything's going to be fine and I have
the best surgeon in the city. So I asked her, what
would she recommend I do if it turns out to be
cancer? She said not to imagine things. That the
surgeon knows best and it would be over soon and
I could go home in a few days."

"She's right. No point in getting upset when you
don't know if there's anything to be upset about."

"Why can't anyone say the word cancer! Why
did they rush me in here like this if there isn't
anything to get upset about?"

"I don't know. They know what they're doing.
Do you need anything? Could I bring you some
grapes or something?"

"No, I'm fine, Elizabeth. I don't need anything.
I'm starving right now. I haven't had anything to
eat since last night."

I felt horrible when I got off the phone. I know
I'm letting her down. But I'm so scared. I know it
isn't cancer. It can't be. But what if it is? It's the
waiting that's driving me crazy. The suspense. The
doctors say it isn't anything serious, but how do
they know? Why is she in hospital and why are
they doing a biopsy, if it isn't serious?

I bought her Christmas present yesterday. I
hope she likes it. I splurged. I got her eight blank

videos and a little stand to keep them in. She likes
to watch documentaries and now she can tape
them and watch them anytime she likes.

I wish I could buy her a car. Then she wouldn't
freeze to death at the bus stop. And I wish I could
buy her a house, so she can plant a garden. She
adores flowers, all kinds, even carnations and
those lilies of the valley that make me think of
funerals. I know if she had a house she'd make
the whole backyard into a garden of flowers, every
kind in the world. She doesn't deserve this. It isn't
fair.

She would love living in a house. I'd buy one
with a large kitchen so she could put the freezer
there. A car and a house. Is that asking for so
much? She deserves it. She's worked hard all her
life and cared for people and

The phone. I don't want to answer it. What if it's
bad news.

"Hello...yes, yes, that's me, how is she?...Is it,
did they, I mean, is she all right? You're sure?
Thank you. Thank you for phoning. Thank you.
Tell her, please, would you, that I'll be in after
supper to see her. Tell her I'll bring some grapes...
Yes, thank you for calling."

Why am I crying again?

Tea For Thirteen

It started off innocently enough, as things often do. Every nine months or so I get the urge to have some friends over. There's nothing profound about the nine months. It has nothing to do with birth or rebirth or gestation. It just works out that way, that's all.

I like to socialize, but women mostly get together for evening parties. They drink and dance and generally make merry under artificial light. Man-made light makes me drowsy, makes me want to fall into a soft bed, and snuggle under a warm layer of bedclothes. Just thinking about it makes me yawn.

Late morning brunches were popular for a while, but that didn't last. Such a shame, I think. I like mornings best, especially sunny mornings. The day is young and filled with promise. I liked going to brunches, but I could never put on a brunch myself. Just think of the work involved. I'd have to cook eggs, not merely scrambled but Benedict or Florentine, and sausages, salmon patties, hot rolls, and fried potatoes. And freshly squeezed orange juice is compulsory. Then there's the piles of dirty dishes and cutlery and pots and pans to wash and dry! Disaster City. Where's the fun in that?

I figured I'd found the perfect solution when I came up with the idea of a tea party. Consider the advantages. Fifteen minutes of preparation is all it takes, twenty at the most. I put out a few pickles and some olives, make a plateful of sandwiches, and pour boiling water over the tea bags. Nothing to it. At my first tea party a couple of women asked for coffee, but I told them I didn't have any coffee and that was that.

The best part is, there aren't any dishes to wash up afterwards, just a few mugs and spoons. Not to forget daylight. A tea party is held in daylight. Even if the tea party lingers into the late afternoon, when the promise of a day is fading, it's still naturally light.

There's another advantage to tea parties. You drink tea instead of alcohol. It's not a big deal. I have a beer sometimes. But alcohol and cigarettes, that stuff hurts women and I'm not in favour of anything that hurts women, that's all. A tea party is perfect, though, because no one expects alcohol. Cigarettes–well, those that use them smoke almost everywhere.

A tea party is a womanly thing. Imagine sitting graciously with a tea cup in one hand (although I use mugs), and a sandwich in the other hand and a dainty napkin across the lap. It brings to mind ladies having cosy conversations, don't you think?

Not that my friends are ladies. No. Most of them wear trousers, and they all work to support themselves. Except Maureen. She doesn't work. She and her two daughters live on social assistance. She doesn't get alimony from her ex.

That's what she calls him, her X, like he was a cross to bear. She makes me laugh. I guess Maureen doesn't qualify as a lady, either. I mean, a lady doesn't live on social assistance, which is welfare when you get right down to it. Welfare means poor, dirt poor. It's not lady-like at all.

Don't get me wrong. I'm not one of those feminists. I know a few and I agree with some of that stuff. But they go too far, don't you think? Take that equal pay business. My Aunt Susan's got a real thing about that one. But I don't buy it. Equal pay? What's equal? I've worked at the same job for ten years now and I work damned hard. My boss, he arrived two years ago and he does nothing all day long. Not a tap of work. He talks to the guys down the hall and takes three-hour lunches, comes in late, leaves early. On Fridays he usually doesn't bother to come in at all. Not that I miss him. But I work hard and do a full day of work and he makes three times as much as I do.

My Aunt Susan never shuts up about that stuff. I told her, men have got to make more money than women. They've got their pride. She didn't like that. She's a feminist. She's the one that told me to stop calling them "libbers". She says that's a put-down, and she expects more from an intelligent woman like me. I like it when she calls me a woman.

She's not a lady, either. She works as a cleaner in a high-rise building downtown. I mean, cleaning offices is not lady-like behaviour.

We argue a lot, Aunt Susan and me. She's almost twice my age, so you can imagine she can out talk me most of the time. She's been around a lot longer. When I said men have got to make more money, because of their pride, she said the cost of groceries and rent is the same for women and men.

"But that's different. I mean, men have got to work to support their families."

"Elizabeth, you amaze me. You think I work because I love my job? For the good of my health maybe? I work because I need to work. Most of us work because we need to, to support ourselves. You, of all people, should know that. I don't see a man paying your bills. Look at your friends. Lesbians don't have men supporting them. Of course, a lot of straight women don't either. Look at me. And look at your friend Maureen. I don't see her husband supporting her and the kids."

What could I say? She's got an answer for everything, my Aunt Susan does. But I'm a fighter and I keep trying. So I said, "I don't believe in abortion."

That's all I said, but she shrieked.

"Elizabeth! No one's asking you to believe. The issue is choice. You've got to have a choice. But," she said in her most serious voice, "the real issue isn't abortion or equal pay, it's choice in everything!"

I've learned to stop talking when she uses her most serious voice. The next step is for her to start yelling at me, and I hate it when people yell, don't you? She takes this feminist stuff too seriously. The best thing to do is to change the subject. So I invited her to my third tea party. That took her mind off choice. But she couldn't come. I was disappointed. She's one of my favourite people.

I couldn't change the date because I'd already invited all sorts of women to the tea party. It was on October 31st, which was a Saturday. Halloween and, wouldn't you know it, a total of twelve women came. Which makes thirteen,

including me. The number didn't mean much to me
at first. Not until long after Karen arrived, carrying
that paper bag. There were five women present by
that time, sitting in my living room with mugs of
tea, all talking merrily. But the room got quiet when
Karen walked in.

She wasn't one of my friends. She was new in
town and Maureen invited her to come so she could
meet some lesbians. Not that I minded. I like to
meet new women and introduce them around so
they get to know other women. But Karen became
the centre of attention at my party.

I started to worry when she took six candles out
of the paper bag. Two blue, two white, and two red.
As she took them out, she announced it was
Hallowmas. "It's a sacred time for women," she said.

I raised my eyebrows at that. "What's sacred
about Halloween?"

"Hallowmas is the women's new year," Karen
said.

I started to feel funny. What was going on? I'd
planned a friendly tea party. I mean, this
Hallowmas business sounded like feminist stuff.
They go in for that kind of thing, have you noticed?
Karen placed the candles in a circle on my glass
coffee table, two blue, two white, and two red. But
in the circle they went blue, white, red, blue, white,
red.

"Are the candles important?" I asked politely,
trying to make the best of it.

She lit the candles, one by one. "The red is most
important. It represents death. This is the time of
death, the coming of winter."

Death. Death! Disaster City. My tea party was
going to be ruined, I mean completely ruined by
this woman with her death candles.

She lit the last candle. "Blue is for friendship. White is for peace. This combination of blue and white and red is for success." She took some incense from the paper bag and set it in an empty ashtray.

I was wondering what else she had in that paper bag.

A knock at the door interrupted the silence. Two more women entered. One of them said, "Hey Karen, how are you? Haven't seen you in a long time. I hear you moved here. What's with the candles? You still into that?"

Karen smiled. I liked her smile. I just thought she was weird, that's all.

"So we can join energy," she said to them, "to celebrate Hallowmas."

"Would you like some tea," I asked the newcomers. I turned to the seated women. "Would anyone like tea?" I learned that in Home Ec, to say would you like some tea, not, would you like some *more* tea. *More* sounds greedy or something.

Four more women arrived, together, all at once. Everyone started talking. I fled to the kitchen. Wouldn't you know it. Karen followed me.

I took four mugs from the cupboard. We were thirteen now. I knew because I have fifteen mugs, so if more than fifteen women came then I'd have to borrow mugs from the woman across the hall.

"Do you have comfrey tea?"

This woman was one surprise after another. What is comfrey tea? "No," I said. "I have Red Rose."

"It doesn't matter. The ceremony is what's important."

The ceremony? She must be a feminist, though I didn't know what candles and ceremonies and

comfrey tea had to do with it. It looked like I was
going to find out, whether I wanted to or not.
Don't get me wrong. I have an open mind. I try
new things. This was weird, that's all. I don't like
weird things.

"Do you know my Aunt Susan?"

"No, I don't know many women here yet."

Karen helped me carry the teapot and mugs to
the living room. She poured while I handed out
the mugs. She had good-looking hair, reddish and
curly, sticking out all over. I liked her hands. I
notice hands. Hers had long fingers. She held my
teapot with both hands, her long fingers circling
the roundness, as if it were a work of art. I got it
for thirteen ninety-five in the basement of Zellers.
Maybe I'd buy some comfrey tea for the next tea
party. Not because she liked it or anything. I like
to try new things.

I looked over at Maureen. She was sitting back,
watching Karen too. She looked flabbergasted, like
I felt. Maureen and I agree about all that feminist
stuff. She looked at me and rolled her eyes to the
ceiling.

"Shall we begin? Is everyone comfortable?" The
room got quiet and everyone looked at Karen.
"This is not a true ceremony. The tradition of
witches places ceremonies outside. But we can
still have a celebration for Hallowmas indoors."

She was a witch! And I thought she was a
feminist. Aunt Susan never said anything about
witches. I'd remember something like that. I would
have to ask Aunt Susan about witches.

"Everyone gather close to the coffee table, in a
circle, and join hands." Karen lit the incense and
the rest of us followed her instructions. We edged
forward, toward those six flickering flames. I

managed to seat myself beside Karen. I needed to be close by, to keep an eye on her.

She took my hand and held it in a firm grip. I like a firm grip, not someone hanging on to my hand like it was a dead fish. I find assertive women very attractive. This one was assertive with a capital A. She had taken over my tea party and turned it into a Hallowmas celebration!

She told us to close our eyes and empty our minds, completely empty our minds. No one's ever told me to empty my mind and I didn't know how to begin. I tried. I really did. I must have an awfully full mind, because I couldn't get it empty.

I wondered if any of the other women had the same problem. I opened my eyes and looked around the circle, quickly, then closed them again. Was Maureen sitting there with a completely empty mind? Since I couldn't get my mind empty, I thought about Karen's hand and wondered who gave her the ring on her second finger. It was cutting into my hand ever so slightly.

She told us to open our eyes and concentrate on a candle flame. That wasn't difficult. I didn't mind watching the flame grow and shrink. It was fascinating. Until I noticed that my candle was blue and remembered that blue represents friendship, and then I felt Karen's hand holding mine and her ring pressing into my hand and lost my concentration. This concentration stuff wasn't as easy as it sounded.

Karen spoke again. She told us to close our eyes again and think about the past year, and then to envision what we wanted for the coming year. That was the easiest part. I skipped the past year. It was over. I mean, what's the point in thinking about it. I prefer to concentrate on the future.

I envisioned a new car in the garage. It took a couple of minutes to decide between a Corvette and a Porsche, but I finally went for a vintage red Corvette with white leather upholstery. Then I envisioned a green leather couch with matching chair and footstool in the living room, a painting by Mary Meigs on the wall above the couch, I like her books, and a Canada Savings Bond for twenty thousand in the top drawer of my bureau. I went through my closet and added a few flashy clothes to go with the Corvette.

I wondered what the other women were thinking. I was getting the hang of this and it was fun. But it wasn't like any party I'd ever been to.

I went back to concentrating on the future. I envisioned Maureen winning a lottery and buying a big old house in the country, and giving the kids piano lessons and ski equipment.

Just as I was beginning to envision Maureen building a house down the road from her for my Aunt Susan, I was in the midst of planning the layout of the rooms, Karen interrupted. She told us to think about ourselves, about our own bodies and the earthly bodies around us. She said some words about the goddess and seasons changing and internal strength. I could have listened to her forever. But as far as ceremonies go, nothing happened!

Afterwards, after Karen had put out the candles, we all sat in the circle, not knowing whether to talk or what.

Maureen giggled and ended the silence. "That was fun. I feel relaxed."

Everyone laughed, even Karen. Conversations started up. I escaped to the kitchen, to make tea. Karen followed me again.

"How do you feel?"

"Good. I'm calm."

"Do you feel centred?"

Centred? Now what on earth did that mean. I smiled at her. "I suppose I do."

"There were thirteen in the circle. Thirteen women."

"I know."

"You noticed we were thirteen? It's a lucky number. Did you know that?"

What could I say. "Are you a witch?"

Karen nodded. "Sure! You are too. We all are, all women."

"I'm not a witch." How could she say something like that. I'd know if I was a witch. It's the sort of thing you'd know.

Karen smiled. I wanted her to keep smiling at me. "We are all witches. Some of us don't think about it, but we all are." She picked up my teapot, with both hands again. "How'd you really feel during the ceremony?"

I grinned. Grinning's more my style. "Calm. I felt calm when it was over. When it was happening, I kept wondering what would happen next and what the others were thinking about."

"You're honest, aren't you. Concentration takes practice." She was still smiling. "Are you making more tea?"

"Yup. Could you get the tray from the living room. The pitcher will need more milk."

I filled the kettle and plugged it in, then tidied the kitchen counter while she was gone. Why did she say that, that I'm honest? I had to admit, I was attracted to her. Even if she did think she was a witch. I like women who are different. They keep life fun.

As the kettle started to boil, she came back with the tray. "They're talking about ESP in the living room. And about women's intuition." She looked pleased.

I had other things on my mind. "Do you want to stay for supper?" I'm not slow when it comes to women.

She smiled. I like that smile.

"I'd love to. I'll help you clean up when the others leave."

Cleaning up wasn't going to take long. "I'd appreciate that." Then I had second thoughts. I can be impulsive. Women hit me that way, and it's made trouble for me once or twice. "Do you have anything else in that brown bag?"

She laughed. I like her laugh.

She said I needed a witch name. I didn't know
what to say, although I am not usually at a loss
for words.

We'd been going together for a few weeks at
that point. I didn't really know her. We were
almost strangers, you could say. I knew parts of
her, though. I knew she liked ear kisses. Yes she
does. Wet lips circling her ear. She likes that
almost as much as mouth kisses. Mouths
kissing. I like that word, kissing.

I knew from the start that she was different,
and I liked her for it. I figured I could live with her
weirdness. I was interested in finding out.

When she said I needed a witch name, I
decided to go along with her. What harm could it
do?

"How do I get a witch name?"

I knew she was a witch from when I first met
her. She told me, as if it was the sort of thing to
make a woman feel pride. But that didn't stop me
from taking her in my arms, and taking her to my
bed. I felt a powerful attraction to her. That first
night I watched her hands massaging my belly
and I forgot everything else in the world.

"There are various ways. A name could come to you, a name that seems right."

"My mind is a blank."

"Well, see, you could look at the runic alphabet and see if any letters speak to you."

Runic alphabet? I don't remember any mention of that when I was in school. She sure is weird.

"Let's try that."

She takes one of her witch books from the bookcase and sits beside me on the sofa. I adore her hands. The book rests on one knee and her thumb tickles the pages, fanning them with a stroking motion. I wish her thumb was tickling me.

"Are you ready?"

She makes everything into a ceremony. Before she comes to bed, she opens the window and looks out at the stars. Then she stretches. I always try to get into bed while she's opening the window and staring at the stars, so I can watch her stretch. On cold nights she wears a t-shirt but I don't mind. I can see her breasts stretching beneath the cloth.

"Sure."

She opens the book slowly, balancing the spine of the book in her left palm.

"This is the ancient language of witches, this alphabet." She leafs through the pages, looking for a particular page.

After she stretches, she sets the alarm clock. Every night she places it gently on the night table and turns to me with a smile. I adore her smile. This is my favourite part. In a moment she will be in bed, snuggling against me. I'll give her ear kisses, little ones along the edge. It makes her giggle.

"Here," she says, and I look at the page. "You can pick some letters and put them together in a name."

What are these strange letters? What will I do with a witch name? If I whisper it as I kiss her ear, will she love me even more? I want to make her love me more than she loves anyone, more than she has ever loved in her life.

"Should I pick any letters at all?"

She smiles at me. "Well, see, if you concentrate then certain letters will come to you. They'll be your letters and form your name."

I want to give her ear kisses right now, to make her close the book and balance my breasts in the palms of her hands. I want to place my hands on her back, to feel the hum of her body as I knead the skin.

"Maybe I should hold the book."

She gives it to me and our fingers touch. Her fingers are warm. I'll do this. I'll pick some letters. Once it's over, I'll put my arms around her and kiss her on the mouth.

"Are any letters coming to you?"

She likes to wrap her legs around my hips and squeeze. The first time she did it, I wondered if she'd done it to anyone before. I asked her. She said everything is new between us. That's how I feel too. There's never been anyone like her.

"Yes. This one and this one, and this." I'm hurrying. I want to get it over with.

She seems excited. "Let's see what they spell."

I don't care. This is her ceremony. I want to get on to the good stuff, to fingers and wet chins and orgasms. That's my kind of ceremony.

"Bir." She looks at me. "They spell Bir."

Sometimes I wonder if it will change. One night

she will forget to stretch and I'll be too tired to give her ear kisses. I want to hold on to her, hold so tight she can't ever get away.

"It suits you. Bir."

It does? Bur? They're prickly things that catch on your socks when you walk through the bush.

"Do you have a witch name?"

"Of course."

Of course. As if everyone does. That's part of her weirdness. She sees the world a little differently from the way the rest of us do. "What is it?"

"Danci."

That makes me laugh. It suits her.

One night she cried in my arms, because she couldn't make the orgasm come. I told her that she wanted it too much. She's greedy that way, wanting an orgasm every time, sometimes two. She held me tightly while she cried. I thought she'd never stop. I told her she was too sexy for words, and what was one orgasm in a lifetime. That made her smile.

I put my arms around her. "Bir and Danci, that's me and you!"

She laughs and then I feel her lips on mine.

Lies At Lunch

"I'll buy you lunch," Karen says, holding the door open for me.

"Thanks." I step inside, avoiding her eyes. I know without looking that she has beautiful eyes. Vivid blue, outlined by long reddish lashes.

I stand behind her in the line, staring up at the overhead menu, wondering which delicacies to choose. Why is it so difficult to decide what to have when the menu offers such a limited selection?

Karen doesn't have much money these days and that makes her invitation all the more special. Why am I letting such a simple thing like an invitation to lunch bother me?

I think I've been thinking too much lately. That's the problem. I don't know what started me off this time. Maybe it was the conversation with my Aunt Susan.

Whatever started it, it's here, this thought. It's like a little seed that's been planted in my brain and it's grown roots and I can't shake it loose. I want to know, just how honest can you be with the love of your life? This question has taken hold of my brain and no matter how hard I try I just can't stop thinking about it.

Picture this. Two goblets of white wine. The flickering flame from the candle is reflected in the round glass. The black-eyed waitress has a musical accent and a friendly smile. Quiet Muzak plays in the background, mingled with murmurs of gentle conversation from other diners. Doesn't that feel divine?

Forget it. Karen is buying me lunch at Wendy's. This is not, I repeat, *not* my idea of being taken out to lunch. Dare I tell her?

It's a trivial thing, isn't it, where we have lunch. There are bigger things, more important issues to worry about. But this one, minor as it seems, is bothering me more than I can say.

I want to be open and honest with my love and my friends and my family. But what is worth saying? How can I know when to be truthful and when to be silent? When does silence mean discretion and when is it deceit?

I was out for years before I told my family I am a lesbian. I thought I was being discreet. Last week my Aunt Susan told me I had been lying.

"You lied to me all those years when you didn't tell me you are a dyke," she said. "An omission is the same as telling a lie."

"A lie? You think I lied to you?" I didn't mean to lie. I just didn't want to make trouble for myself.

(Tell me this. Does that mean I was lying to her last year when I didn't tell her that her new red sofa is the ugliest piece of furniture I have ever seen? Maybe not the ugliest, but it sure is ugly. It's comfortable to sit on, I'll say that much. But the style is ultra modern and the colour makes me think of raw liver. I hate liver, raw or cooked. I didn't tell her the truth. Instead, I said, "It's a comfy sofa.")

I said, "You never told me you were straight, so why should I tell you I'm not?" I mean, I had to defend myself. Nobody likes to be called a liar.

I have to admit, I was tempted to say, "And besides if you want to know the truth about everything then you should know that this is one ugly sofa." I wanted to say that because my feelings were hurt and I wanted to hurt her back. There was no reason to say it, except to hurt her but I know that's not a reason to speak the truth. I mean, I don't have to live with the sofa. How I feel about that liver sofa doesn't really matter.

We were sitting in her living room, both of us on the ugly sofa. She didn't say anything, which surprised me. It's not easy to silence my Aunt Susan.

Finally she said, "You have a point, Elizabeth."

I didn't mean to shut her up. I didn't want to make a point. I just didn't want her calling me a liar.

"So do you," I said. "Everybody goes around assuming everyone is straight. Being a lesbian is important. So it was like living a lie, not telling you. I'm sorry."

She took my hand and kissed the tip of each finger. I could have cried. It makes me feel so good when she does that. She doesn't do it very often, but when she does it thrills me.

"I confess, I don't know what it's like, Elizabeth, to be a lesbian in this straight world."

Is it any wonder that I love her? She's my best friend, has been since I was a kid. Even if she is a straight woman.

Then she said, "But I was hurt that you didn't tell me. Don't you trust me?"

Well, I felt awful. First she thinks I'm a liar and now she thinks I don't trust her. I tried to make myself feel better by telling myself that she doesn't understand. A woman who's been straight all her life and lived with heterosexual privilege, she can't possibly understand what it's like. No matter how hard she tries and how much she cares about me. She can't know how unsafe it is for me in this world.

Maybe that's where it started, all this thinking about lies and being open to those I care about. I'm glad Aunt Susan confronted me. Even if it did make me feel like I should go sit in a garbage pail and repeat over and over, I am a bad person.

But my Aunt Susan doesn't know about the risks. I sat there on the ugly liver sofa and tried to tell her. I told her that Nancy's parents disowned her and kicked her out of the family. They said they never wanted to see her again. They meant it. Nancy hasn't seen her family for fifteen years.

I reminded her that Maureen's ex tried to take the kids away from her. He yelled and used foul language and threatened Maureen for months. No court would let a lesbian near her daughters, he said. She lived with fear. The only reason she still has her daughters is that he's too lazy to follow through on anything. He still threatens her when he wants to get his own way. He's a creep so he doesn't have any second thoughts about blackmailing her. Like when he wanted to take the girls to his parents for Christmas this year. He had them for Christmas last year and the year before last. And they spent Christmas with his parents again this year. Maureen gives in because she knows it is quite possible the court would take her daughters away, simply because she is a lesbian. A legal fight would leave her deep in debt for the rest of her life. And, whether she won or lost, she fears that a court battle would scar her children.

I told Aunt Susan that even if I think I know someone, I can't be sure of how any person will respond when I come out. To trust someone completely is asking a great deal. You know what I mean? When a woman tells her parents that she's a dyke, she doesn't expect to wake up in a psych unit the next morning. That's what happened to Ellie. Aunt Susan knows Ellie. She works at the women's bookstore, and Aunt Susan is in there at least once a month.

Those doctors and nurses locked Ellie away and tortured her for months, with her parents' approval. She says her parents had good intentions and that they love her, in their own way. I wouldn't be so forgiving. The way I see it, it's a perverted kind of love if you think seizures induced by bolts of electricity combined with massive doses of mind-altering drugs are better for your daughter than having her care deeply for another woman. What a horrible thing to do to your daughter. It's frightening. And if you can't trust your parents, who can you trust?

Nothing awful happened to me. I was over thirty when I came out to my parents, and I had been making my own way in the world for years. Although they were not pleased, let me tell you. They didn't really say anything, but I could read the signs. At family gatherings I noticed my mother stopped telling everyone I was too young to settle down. Even now, when she phones to invite me to Sunday dinner she never invites Karen. I bring Karen anyway. And every time I mention a friend, or bring someone over to their house, the first thing my father asks me is, "Is she married?"

(And I know he means, Is she married to a *man*.)

I know they were expecting a son-in-law and grandchildren. Parents get some peculiar ideas. I mean, can you picture me with a husband and children? It boggles the mind. But my parents are adjusting. Last year my mother bought Karen a Christmas present. It's taking time, but these things often do I've noticed.

I have learned the truth is sometimes dangerous.

Being a lesbian has made lots of trouble for me. I've seen an employer get angry, and then watched the anger turn to heat. He drove me crazy for two years. He was always brushing against me and bringing his face close to mine when he talked to me. His breath was foul. I was tempted to leave a bottle of mouthwash on his desk. But that would only clean a small part of him.

He kept nagging me to go out to dinner with him. He hadn't shown any interest in me until he found out I was a lesbian. I could tell what was going on in his filthy mind. Straight men are turned on by lesbians. It comes of reading porn from the time they're old enough to turn the pages of a glossy magazine. You don't believe me, take a look at some porn. It's filled with so-called lesbians being saved by naked men with big cocks. Triple yuck.

Because I wouldn't go along with his disgusting fantasy, he fired me. He said I was incompetent. I was the bookkeeper and I'd been doing my job, with no complaints, for ten years. How did I suddenly become incompetent?

On my last day I looked him right in the eye, standing back to avoid his smelly breath, and yelled, "You're a liar and we both know it. This will come back to haunt you one day, I promise you." It felt so good to confront him and get my anger out.

I hope his wife turns out to be a lesbian. And his mother. And his mistress.

So. I was honest with him. Big deal. It didn't change anything. I was out of a job. He won and he won by lying. Where's the justice? My policy from then on was never come out to straight men.

I was brought up to be truthful about facts. If my mother asked if I'd made my bed or done my homework, I was expected to speak the truth. Actually, I was expected to say yes and heaven help me if that wasn't the truth.

I wasn't expected to say, "Mother, I want to talk to you. The way you criticize me for taking so long to do the dishes and getting water on the floor really hurts my feelings. It makes me feel that I'm not very good at it. And I'd like to discuss it with you."

Can you picture that?

During my formative years, no one taught me to be truthful about feelings. I was brought up to be a good girl, to be polite to others, never raise my voice. Don't get me wrong. I'm not trying to blame this on anyone else. It's just that I haven't learned how to be truthful about my feelings.

I read a book about it once, about how to communicate openly and honestly. It said a few helpful things like I should say 'I feel' rather than 'You make me feel.' But it's one thing to read about it in a book. It's a whole other thing to do it in my life.

I tried it with Karen.

I said to her, after I read that book, "I feel unimportant when you tell our friends that the only thing I know how to cook is scrambled eggs. I feel like you don't respect me. I feel you're telling them that I'm incompetent."

Karen said, "Don't try to make me feel like a mean person. I never said you were incompetent. Never once have I said that. Have I? Tell me when I said you were incompetent. I didn't make you feel that way and I'm not taking responsibility for how you feel."

That wasn't how she was supposed to respond, according to the book. It said I must keep myself open so I was supposed to say, "It is hard for me to say this. I'm afraid of hurting you and afraid of you hurting me. But you deserve to know how I feel. I need you to know."

Instead, I said, "Damn you! Don't twist my words. Just listen to me and don't jump down my throat. I never said *you* make me feel that way. I said that was how I felt!"

The conversation was downhill from there on, and then we didn't talk to each other for three whole days. What a mess. I mean, it hardly encourages me to talk about how I feel, does it.

Cooking is not worth the bother. If I may be honest, I hate cooking. It's an activity that simply does not interest me. Eating is all right. I like eating. And, of course, eating is essential to life. But cooking, that bores me.

I have to admit, cooking has its uses. Imagine what a revolutionary act it would be if women all over the world refused to cook for a month. We could say, Disarm all nuclear weapons or we'll never cook again. One month is all it would take. The power women have in our own precious hands.

Unfortunately, the world would be grateful if I stopped cooking for a month. The whole world except Karen.

Why do I feel like I'm some kind of unnatural woman because I don't like to cook? Karen doesn't like skating but nobody thinks any less of her for it.

This is complex, have you noticed? If we can't come to any kind of understanding about cooking, where does that leave us? What does it say about our relationship? I never want to eat what I cook and, if everyone else is being honest, they don't want to either. I'm just not inclined that way. Why can't Karen accept that about me?

She knows I detest cooking, but she still expects me to make my share of meals. Just my luck, she doesn't think a peanut butter sandwich is a meal. I'm also partial to beans on toast, but she turns her nose up at that too. She's a fussy eater.

I know the look she gets in her eyes when I try to talk to her about cooking. Those warm blue eyes turn cold and fierce. Her laughing mouth, so full and friendly, becomes a thin line. Talking about it just doesn't get us anywhere. I don't understand why she can't understand my point of view.

She got that look in her eyes last February, when I told her I was disappointed that she didn't get me anything for Valentine's Day. Not so much as one chocolate, not one flower, not one mushy card.

I didn't even think before I spoke. "My heart is broken."

She took off her coat and boots and said, "Don't hand me that. You want me to celebrate some fool man who was made a saint by some other fool men in long gowns? What does your heart have to do with them?"

I felt tears in my eyes. I was so upset I didn't try to stop my tears. Was I asking for much? I just wanted her to declare her love for me, not to worship some dead man. I wanted her to show me that she loved me by buying me a box of chocolates.

When you look at it like that, it sounds pretty trivial. A box of chocolates. It doesn't compare with the week I was so sick I couldn't get out of bed to go to the bathroom and Karen stayed home with me. She gave me a bath in bed, and fed me sips of flat ginger ale, and sat in our bedroom for hours with her arms around me while I dozed. She brought the newspaper in and read it to me, even the hockey scores.

Can't I have chocolates once a year too? Tell me honestly, is that asking too much?

I tried to clear my throat and muttered, "It's a tradition and you know it." By this time tears were streaming down my face. "No one cares about Saint Valentine. He's nothing. It's a special day for sweethearts! Aren't we sweethearts?"

I started sobbing. I was disappointed in myself. It's hard to win an argument when you're crying uncontrollably. It's not that I wanted to win. Don't get me wrong. That's just a figure of speech. I wanted to be taken seriously. I wanted to be listened to, that's all.

She got me some tissue and put her arms around me. "It's bad enough that you expect me to celebrate Christmas. I'm not even a Christian. Neither are you. Think about it, Elizabeth."

I've learned that when she tells me to think about it, she doesn't want me to think at all. She wants me to listen.

"I've got to get out of these clothes and have a shower." She threw my crumpled tissue in the garbage and came back to sit beside me. "Some man is born two thousand years ago and makes a martyr of himself and we're expected to make a big fuss about it every year. Sure, he was a humanitarian. But there have been lots of humanitarians over the centuries. What I can't figure out is how he persuaded his mother, and don't you think she must have been a martyr herself, to agree to his story of the virgin conception. Of course, maybe it suited her purposes too. Maybe getting pregnant without being married was grounds for being stoned to death. The only way around it was being impregnated by God via an angel. Maybe it was all her idea. Aren't women inventive!"

If you think that's all she had to say, you don't know Karen. She handed me the box of tissues and continued talking.

"If we're going to celebrate the birth of some dead martyr, why not Joan of Arc? She was burned to death for being an uppity woman. She refused to wear a dress, no matter how they tortured her. She was a better warrior than all the men, and an expert on military strategy. Now that's someone worth making a fuss about."

These feminists. They take all the fun out of life. I've been enjoying Valentine's Day ever since I can remember. But do they care? They want to change everything in the whole world, have you noticed? They rant and rave, but if you ask me they're confused. I mean, they're always going on about disarmament, yet they worship a woman for being a great warrior. Where's the sense in that?

How come I feel like an awful woman for wanting Karen to give me a few measly chocolates on February fourteenth? And I noticed that little jab about wearing dresses.

I thought about putting my arms around her and resting my cheek against her cheek, so she could feel the tears of my sorrow and remember my love. I thought about staring at her, with my anger blazing, and pulling her nose until it stretched inches from her pinched face and brought tears of pain to her eyes. My feelings were all jumbled.

I didn't want to upset her. But I was upset and didn't she need to know how I felt? Wouldn't that help us to understand one another better, be more aware of our needs, and enjoy a more satisfying relationship? That's what the book said.

I know she cares about my feelings, but sometimes she acts like she doesn't. Sometimes she ignores my feelings and refuses to listen to me. Sometimes she says, "I don't have time to talk about it right now." Other times she listens and says, "I don't understand you at all." And sometimes she says, "I love you," and I know she means it.

Wasn't this the time to be truthful or honest or whatever it is that I needed to be? I'm willing to compromise. I'm a reasonable woman. I blew my nose, making a sound like a tired tuba. "If I find out when Joan of Arc was born, will you give me chocolates on that day?"

She laughed. "This is important to you, isn't it." She gave me another hug. "I'm getting changed. I'll make supper tonight." She went off to the bedroom to put on her jeans and a t-shirt.

The next evening, February fifteenth, she came home with two bags of oranges from the fruit and vegetable store. The price was on the bags, $3.89 each. She made two large glasses of real orange juice from all those oranges. I was amazed that she spent that much money, when she could buy a jug of reconstituted juice for much less. It was her way of apologizing and I appreciated it. But it wasn't the same. I mean a glass of orange juice on February fifteenth, even if it is freshly-squeezed, is just not the same as a heart-shaped box of chocolates on February fourteenth. Do you know what I mean?

So here I am in Wendy's, trying to appear grateful once again. I'm not thankful for this square patty of hamburger. And to make it worse, I feel guilty because I'm not one bit grateful. Why couldn't we eat at that crêpe place in the Market or the Indian restaurant on Rideau Street?

Instead, our food is in styrofoam containers, on a plastic tray. And there's a paper place mat with a question across the top in large black letters. EVER WONDERED WHO WENDY IS? Who cares.

Maybe how important something or someone is to me in my life is a sign of how much I care. Is it important to tell the love of my life that I feel hurt when she criticizes me for wearing dresses to work? It comes up every so often, like her comment about Joan of Arc refusing to wear dresses six centuries ago. Let's face it, I'm no Joan of Arc. All the women wear dresses where I work. I have to do it to fit in and get ahead. Why can't Karen understand that? Sometimes feminists go too far. She makes me feel like a coward and a traitor. But I've got to do what I've got to do for my career.

Sometimes I have to say what I'm feeling. I can't help myself. "Look, Karen, I'm not happy eating at Wendy's."

Karen speaks before I can say another word. "I know, I know, neither am I. It's shameful. We've made a mistake."

Shameful? I wouldn't go so far as to say that. It's not very romantic. But shameful?

She sticks the white plastic spoon in the chili and looks disgusted. "We shouldn't be here. Rain forests in South America are being destroyed to produce beef for greedy people like us. It's just that it was convenient and fast to stop here. You were right to say something. Let's leave this so-called food. We'll eat somewhere else. Do you have any ideas?"

It takes me a minute to recover. We've paid for this food. How can we walk away from it? That would be a waste of money and food. Don't you think a feminist would be against wasting food? I don't care. It will be worth it, to pay more money for some real food.

I stand up, grinning. "Let's go to the vegetarian restaurant. You like their veggie and nut loaf. It'll be my treat. I'll take you to lunch."

"No," she said. "I want to buy you lunch."

"You did. Now it's my turn. It'll give me more pleasure than you can imagine."

We link arms as we walk through the noisy restaurant. I feel light-hearted and want to sing. La la la...Shall I tell her that I was thinking of romance rather than tropical rain forests?

Maybe, when we are sitting at the vegetarian restaurant, I'll try again. I'll tell her that I have good reasons for wearing dresses, and I'd like to explain my reasons if she feels like listening. I want her to listen. I need her to listen with an open mind. Sometimes I feel like she doesn't respect me and my reasons. It hurts. That's the truth. I feel hurt when I think she doesn't respect me.

If she starts yelling that she's never said she

doesn't respect me, I'll let her yell. Sooner or later she'll stop. Then we'll talk some more. I won't let the silence and hatred grow between us for three days this time. We'll do it differently. I'll beg her, if I have to, to talk to me. I'll promise to listen to her and ask her to listen to me.

As we walk along the street I look over at her blue eyes and feel such a rush of emotion that I squeeze her arm. "I love you." She smiles at me.

One thing I have learned through the years: you can't have everything. But that never stops me.

The next time I'm near the public library, I'm going in to find out when Joan of Arc was born. I don't suppose Karen will be able to find any Happy Joan-of-Arc-Day cards in the drugstore as the day approaches. I'd prefer a hand-made card anyway.

I won't give up. This is important. After all, I'm going to spend the rest of my life with her. I adore her. Even if she is one of those confused feminists.

With My Little Eye

"She's a plant."

"She? What she?"

"You mean, *which* she."

Kaaaren. I don't want my English corrected! I want to go to sleep. What is she going on about? A plant? Like a geranium? I had a geranium once, a beautiful plant with lush red flowers. I talked to it, watered it, played it nice music, but it died. Plants don't seem to get along with me, even though I like them.

"What do you mean, she's a plant?" I sighed loudly. "I'm tired. Can't we talk about this tomorrow?"

It had been a long day, one of those days when absolutely everything goes wrong. It started when I slept through the alarm and was an hour late for work. I got there and discovered my office was like a sweat box because something was wrong with the damned air conditioning. The minute I sat down at my desk one of the salespeople came into my office and started yelling at me. Shouting from the moment he opened his large mouth. His commission cheque was all wrong this month and he didn't know how I got the job because I was the stupidest bookkeeper he'd ever seen and he was missing thirteen dollars and seventy-two cents and he wanted his money today.

When he paused in his ranting and raving, I smiled at him, my special smile that I keep for special people, and said, "Why don't you go sit in a cold shower."

You can't let these guys walk all over you or they will.

He looked like his eyes were going to pop right out of his head. He screamed that he was going to report me to the boss. He slammed the door so hard that the photograph of Karen fell off the corner of my desk and the glass shattered when it hit the floor. I was tempted to run after him and tell him what I really thought of him.

He doesn't scare me. If the boss says anything to me, I'll say I thought the heat was getting to him and I was giving him a friendly suggestion. What if this guy started yelling at the customers like that? And what right does he have to yell at me? I'll tell the boss that, too.

It was such a busy day that I couldn't find a minute to check through the records to see if he was owed thirteen dollars and seventy-two cents. Maybe I'll have time on Monday. Maybe not.

Then, wouldn't you know it, I ate my lunch at my desk and kept working, to make up for being late, and spilled a glass of iced tea all over the general ledger. What a mess. I felt like screaming. Disaster City.

After a day like that, I couldn't even look forward to going home and putting my feet up.

Maureen was coming to dinner and bringing
someone, so I had to make a special meal.
Maureen is my best friend, next to Karen of
course, and I love sharing good food with her. So I
went home and spent two hours cooking. It was a
nice evening. But it had been one of those days
and now all I wanted to do was sleep.

I'm not in a mood to talk. And why does Karen
want to talk about plants in the middle of the
night? She's weird, but this was a little too weird,
even for her.

"Listen, Elizabeth. She's a *spy*. I'm sure of it."

Sssspy. The word hissed at me in the dark. It
woke me up. I turned over and opened my tired
eyes just wide enough to squint at Karen.

"Did you say she's a spy?"

"Yes."

"A spy? Who's a spy? What are you talking
about?"

Karen smiled. Even in the dark I could see her
white teeth smiling at me. "I thought you were
tired."

"I am." I touched her face.

"I think she's a spy, that woman Maureen
brought to dinner."

"You think Alice is a spy? She seemed like a
pleasant woman. Why would you think such a
thing?" I sat up and pulled the sheet around my
shoulders. This was a bizarre conversation. But
after a day like today, it made complete sense to
have a spy for dinner.

"It's a feeling I have. She didn't say much all
evening, but I had the feeling she was listening
carefully to everything we said and taking mental
notes. And when I asked her what she did, do you
remember, she said she worked for the

government and changed the subject. It was strange. Did you notice that?"

"No." I closed my eyes. "I didn't notice. Who would she be spying for?"

"I've been thinking about that. It could be the RCMP, or maybe that new security service, CSIS. Maybe one of the big corporations. I don't know. It wouldn't be a foreign government. They're too busy spying on each other."

I had a vision of a tiny transmitter hidden behind the picture above our heads, relaying our conversation to a smoke-filled room with men huddled around a table of sophisticated electronic equipment. I opened my eyes. "This sounds unlikely. A spy? Why would anyone want to spy on us?"

"Not us, you and me, but us, the women's movement. Maybe they think we're lesbian agitators."

"Lesbian agitators? Get serious. Not us." I yawned. "Let me think about it. I'm sooooo tired. Let's talk about it in the morning. I've got to get to sleep."

I wiggled down in the bed and turned over. Was Alice sitting in a booth in some dimly-lit bar at this very moment, drinking whiskey and scribbling notes about her evening at our place? It didn't seem possible. Alice wasn't a spy. Karen has a vivid imagination. She should have been a writer. I hope I remember to tell her in the morning. It's not too late to change careers. She's only thirty-nine.

I was the first one up in the morning, as usual. Since it was Saturday, I was drinking my second glass of iced tea and reading the funnies when Karen got up. She stood in the kitchen doorway, not wearing a stitch of clothing and holding her hand over her eyes to ward off the bright sunlight.

"Good morning. I like your body." My next thought was, Is someone listening in on our conversation? I felt an incredible urge to bend down and see if a tiny microphone was attached to the underside of our table.

Karen blew a kiss at me and disappeared into the bathroom.

A few minutes later I heard her footsteps.

"What are you doing?"

I sat up quickly. "Nothing. Just checking to see if the table needs dusting underneath. I never think to look there when I'm cleaning."

She was wearing my dressing gown and carrying two white pills on the palm of her hand. "My head aches. It was that cheap wine. Would you get me some milk?"

I couldn't resist saying, "I don't think it was the quality of the wine, but the quantity." I poured a glass of milk for her. "Poor sweetheart, you look awful."

"I feel awful." She popped the pills into her mouth and drank the milk.

"Perhaps Alice drugged the wine she brought last night."

"Elizabeth! I never thought of that."

"Karen, would you lighten up! I had a glass of that wine and I'm fine. Sappho save us!"

"I'm serious, Elizabeth. I think she's a plant. Don't you believe me?"

"I don't want to talk about it."

I went into the living room and turned on the television. Karen followed me. I wanted some background noise, to make it difficult for anyone to hear what we said. Just in case someone was listening. I'm prepared to say what I think to anyone, but I want to know who I'm saying it to.

What had we talked about last night with Maureen and Alice? I hated the feeling of paranoia that had come over me. I couldn't believe what Karen was saying. A spy in our own house? But I couldn't ignore it, either. What had we talked about? About power, how it corrupts, and how some feminists want control over others to feed their egos. That's a favourite topic of Karen's. She can go on about it for hours. And often does.

And we discussed the Prime Minister and how he has no understanding of the needs and rights of women. I remember asking the others if they thought he was stupid. Or was it that he hated women.

Would Alice report that to someone?

Maureen said, "He's a man," as if that explained it. But that's no excuse. Men can read books and they can listen to women. They can open their eyes and look around. They have imaginations, don't they?

It doesn't take a genius to see that some people have to put up with a lot of shit because of their culture or skin colour. I mean, I'm white and I know that racism exists. Even in me. But I work to change it–in me and around me. And the same things apply to discrimination against women. Acknowledge that oppression exists and work damn hard to erase it. If you have the will it can be done, and it can even be done quickly. The ways to bring about change seem simple to me.

Do you think that means I'm smarter than the Prime Minister?

I'm sure Alice had agreed with us about all that. Could she be talking to the Prime Minister right now, sitting in a plush chair in his air-conditioned office, telling him that I said he was stupid? No.

She wouldn't report directly to the Prime Minister.
I mean, the government's a big bureaucracy. She'd
report to her supervisor and her supervisor would
report to his supervisor and...

Karen sat beside me on the couch and put her
arms around me.

"It's hot already. Want to go out for breakfast?
To some place that's air-conditioned?"

What else had we talked about last night? What
could be used against us? I pressed the button on
the remote control to increase the sound from the
t.v. and hugged Karen back.

"Yes. I'd like to get out of this place." I spoke
very quietly.

She looked surprised. I hate eating out. It's a
waste of good money and the food is usually
overcooked. If it's a nouveau cuisine restaurant
the portions are too small and if it's a regular
place the portions are too large. But all of a
sudden eating out seemed like a great idea.

As I drove to the restaurant, I wondered if I
should ask Karen if she thought we had been
bugged. But her imagination was working
overtime and I didn't want to give her any more
ideas. I glanced over at her. She was unusually
quiet this morning. She's a wonderfully strong-
willed woman and never hesitates to speak her
mind. Maybe it had already occurred to her and
she was trying to spare me.

At the air-conditioned restaurant, it's a decent
one a few blocks from our place that serves
portions just a little too large, I drank
decaffeinated coffee and waited for my order of
scrambled eggs to arrive. Drinking coffee is a bad
habit I've picked up from Karen. I'm not blaming
her for it. Don't get me wrong. I have free will. But

it's so easy to pick up habits from the women you hang around with.

"Talk to me. Tell me why you think Alice is a spy."

Karen put down her cup of coffee and looked at me. "She doesn't know much about the women's movement or feminist issues."

"Big deal. Lots of women don't. Alice seemed very interested. You know coming to terms with feminism is a slow process, done more on a one-to-one level. Exchanging experiences and feelings. And seeing, at an intellectual level, the oppression and restrictions we endure from birth."

Karen laughed. "Listen to you! I never thought I'd see the day."

I had to smile. Until I met Karen, I was not a feminist. But Karen's been a feminist for years and hanging around with her did me in. I was forced to think about it and, you know, it all makes sense when you think about it. When you really look at all the issues, it's obvious that women are discriminated against and it's beyond me how any intelligent person could think otherwise. And Sappho knows I'm no fool.

"Anything else?"

Karen rested her face in her hands. "She admitted she reads Harlequin Romances, when we were talking about books, and she wasn't embarrassed."

"Big deal. Lots of women read Harlequin Romances. It's a billion-dollar industry aimed solely at women."

"Sure. But not feminists. Feminists don't read that garbage."

"That's not true. I used to read them, before I knew you. Not Harlequin Romances, but those

Regency Romances. I still do once in a while. It's escape fiction, that's all. And look at Marylyn. She reads them. She's an educated woman, isn't she. A feminist, and a doctor too. But Marylyn knows enough not to mention it around feminists."

"Marylyn reads Harlequin Romances?"

"Now don't you tell anyone, and don't tell Marylyn that I told you."

Karen laughed. "Marylyn reads Harlequins!" Then she looked very serious. "Elizabeth, it's this feeling I have. Alice doesn't feel like one of us."

"That doesn't make any sense. One of us? There are a lot of us and we're all different. You're saying strange things. You're scaring me. It doesn't make sense. Reading Harlequins, that doesn't mean anything."

"Precisely what doesn't make sense about this?"

"Why would anyone spy on us?"

"You can't be logical about it. Those kinds of agencies are filled with stupid men. They're gun-toting fanatics. They think we're some kind of threat because they think we're dangerous because they think we think like them. So they infiltrate our groups and spy on us. They want to disrupt our organizations and destroy our networks. They want to turn us against each other."

Doesn't she have a vivid imagination. And she has quite a way with words. She should write thrillers. But this conversation was making me nervous. This wasn't a thriller. This was my life.

"Why would they spy on us? We don't harm anyone. We want change, but we're peaceful."

"That doesn't matter to them. These guys don't understand peace. To them, piece means a gun. The police lobby for the return of capital punishment. They believe in violence. They live it. And the RCMP and that new spy agency, they're police. They're threatened by everything."

"But Alice is a woman."

"Yeah. That's scary. Women working against women. But it happens."

My scrambled eggs arrived. I started eating and watched Karen spread orange marmalade on her toast. I couldn't believe this. Did I know a spy? Could Alice be the Mata Hari of our lesbian community? Alice is a nice name. It doesn't sound like a spy's name.

Karen's right. Some women do work against other...I didn't want to think about that.

Karen put down her toast. "You'll notice they don't bother right wing groups. The men that destroyed the Toronto Women's Bookstore and the abortion clinic, you can bet they don't have spies among that group. The police support them and what they're doing."

I swallowed a mouthful of egg. "Okay, okay. Spies do exist. How do we find out if Alice is a spy and what do we do if she is?"

Karen picked up the toast and took a bite. She chewed slowly and looked around the restaurant, then looked at me. "I don't know. If she is a spy, you'd think they'd train her better, so she'd seem more like a real feminist. But then, I guess if they could train her thoroughly, she'd become a real feminist and they wouldn't have a spy anymore. Do you think I'm crazy?"

"You could be. The evidence is pretty flimsy. Let's go with that. How could she do that, spy on other women?"

"It would just be a job to her, like juggling the books is a job to you."

"I don't juggle books, I balance books."

"That's what I meant. It's the same thing."

"It's not the same thing at all!"

Karen stroked the salt shaker with her lovely long fingers and looked at me.

I looked into her eyes. "You think it would just be a job to her, to become friends with us and spy on us? To report what we say and do, the most intimate details of our lives, to some spy supervisor?"

"Maybe she believes she's saving the world. Or at least the country."

"Listen to us, Karen. To *me*. Talking as if she is a spy. We don't know. She may not be one, you know. What shall we do?"

I was having a lot of trouble believing this was possible, that Maureen, my best friend, would bring a spy to our house. Unknowingly, yes, but still. A spy named Alice. She could be spying on Maureen too. It didn't seem real. Yet Karen seemed so sure and I've learned to trust her feelings.

Karen was watching me, not saying anything. She was obviously upset.

"Let's see. What are our choices? We could confront her and get it out in the open."

Karen shook her head. "No. If she was a spy she wouldn't tell us. That would blow her cover. She'd have to deny it."

"Yeah. We don't have any proof. And we can't tell anyone else. It would be awful to start that kind of rumour if she's innocent. We can't tell anyone, not until we have proof. If there is any. How do we prove it?"

Karen stared at her toast. "Why don't we talk to Maureen, and see what she knows about Alice?"

"That's a good idea. That's a place to start."

Our appetites picked up and we finished breakfast. Karen left a tip that amounted to thirty percent of our bill. I pretended not to notice. She says waitresses work hard for very little money and if we can afford to eat out we can afford to supplement their incomes. She calls it sharing the wealth. I don't feel wealthy, but I suppose I am compared to some women. Don't get me wrong. I believe in sharing the wealth. But I think ten percent is more than enough wealth.

I drove to Maureen's place. She lives in a high-rise out in the west end. We didn't talk much in the car. Could someone, a total stranger, be listening to every word we speak? Even in the car?

Where would they put a microphone in the car? I bet with all the high-tech stuff, they've got microphones so small you'd think it was a harmless speck of dust on the dashboard. I turned the radio on and turned the volume up and said to Karen, "I want to hear the weather report and see if this heat wave is going to break soon."

Music was blaring out, deafening both of us. I couldn't take much more of this. I was getting angry. No one was going to make me feel helpless. I had to do something.

I turned off the radio and looked at Karen. "Do you think I'm smarter than the Prime Minister?"

Karen smiled at me. "It's quite possible. You're certainly more honest, without a doubt."

I winked at her and said in a loud voice, "My sources tell me he beats his wife."

"No! That's disgusting."

"Yeah. And there's more."

"What else do your sources say?"

"That he has one particular aide and this guy's

main job is to keep him supplied with hookers. He likes them in his office, late at night. He's greedy. He likes working women in pairs. And the aide that's the pimp, he wears three-piece suits and carries a briefcase and looks just like all the other bureaucrats. He even has an office and a secretary."

"Oh yeah?"

"Yeah. But it's a secret. Don't tell anyone."

Karen laughed. "I won't, I promise. His secret is safe with me."

Would his spies report that to him? This could be fun.

I parked the car. As we walked into Maureen's building, I whispered, "Do you think they bugged the car?"

"I don't know. But I gather that's why we had that conversation about our honourable leader."

"He's not my leader. And he's not an honourable man."

Karen laughed and squeezed my hand.

Maureen was making cookies with her children and the apartment was filled with the warm, rich smell of baking. They live in an air-conditioned building, so the heat from the oven doesn't make much difference. You wouldn't catch me turning on the oven on a day like this for love nor money.

Her youngest cried, "Elizabeth!" As she threw herself at me, I noticed her hands were covered with flour. "We're going to a movie. Want to come?"

I put my arms around her and gave her a hug, wondering if this delightful child was leaving flour all over my shirt. "We'll see, chicken. Karen and I have to go shopping. Our cupboards are bare."

Judy, Maureen's older daughter, grinned as Karen kissed the top of her head.

"How you doing?"

"I'm okay," Judy said. "It's just like you to arrive when we're baking."

Karen laughed. "I can't help it if I have a sweet tooth." She opened her mouth and pointed at a front tooth. "It's this one. Show me yours."

Judy touched her teeth, tapping one after the other, first her upper teeth and then her lower teeth. We all laughed.

Karen and I stood in the kitchen doorway while they went back to making cookies. It's beyond me why it's called a working kitchen. There wasn't room for anyone to take a deep breath, let alone turn around. It must have been designed by someone who never had to work in one.

Karen went directly to the heart of our visit. "Listen, Maureen. We're wondering about that friend of yours, Alice."

Maureen wiped her hands on a tea towel and opened a jar of walnuts. "Isn't she great! I really like her. I enjoyed bringing her to your place. She's coming out and doesn't know many women. It's a confusing time for her, but she's doing okay."

"How did you meet her?" Karen looked at me as she asked the question.

"Didn't I tell you? It's a hoot. I've known her for years, though not well. She's my sister-in-law! She's the younger sister of my ex. He's having a fit. First his wife turns out to be a lesbian, and now his little sister. Some guys have all the luck." She laughed and laughed. "I have my doubts about his new girlfriend too, and so does Alice, but we aren't saying anything to him. He's getting paranoid."

Alice is her sister-in-law! Why hadn't I made the connection? Maureen had mentioned her to me before. Karen glanced at me. She almost looked disappointed. So much for Alice-the-spy. I had to ask one question.

"Where does she work?"

Maureen looked at the jar in her hand. "It's kind of a secret. She's not very proud of her job. She has a contract with the Department of National Defence, editing a magazine they publish. But she's looking for another job. She joined a peace group last year and she's truly uncomfortable about this job."

Karen laughed half-heartedly. "You must bring her over again."

"I will. She liked you both. Want some shortbread cookies? Or some Walnut Delights? I'll put on the kettle and make tea. We're almost finished this last batch. Why don't you make yourselves comfortable in the living room. The air conditioning works best in there, so you'll be cool."

Karen and I sat on the sofa, close together. I was so relieved I felt like dancing. But Karen had put the idea in my head that there were spies among us, and I felt like I'd lost my innocence. It's scary, when you think about it. I didn't want to think about it.

"You were half-right," I whispered to Karen. "Your instincts were working, but a little off base."

She smiled, a sheepish smile, and put her head on my shoulder. "I sure am tired. Let's go to bed early tonight."

"You're tired!" I hoped she noticed the sarcasm in my voice.

She raised her head and looked at me. "Is that proof? Because she's Maureen's sister-in-law? How can we be sure?"

"I don't know. Maybe we just have to trust her."

"But she's working for the Department of Defence. Doesn't the army have spies?"

"Karen. Don't start again with that."

She laughed, my luscious lover with the sweet tooth and the active imagination. "Want to go to the movies with the kids? Let's do it. The theatre will be air-conditioned. I don't feel like shopping today. We can get the groceries on Monday after work."

"Sure. As long as it isn't a spy movie."

Oh Sweet Heart

"I need a name for you," Karen said. She was sitting cross-legged on the kitchen floor, vigorously polishing one of her new shoes with an ancient cotton tea towel.

"I have a name," I said. I was sitting on a chair beside the kitchen table. I was supposed to be writing cheques, but I ignored the small pile of bills and envelopes. I preferred to watch Karen. "I like my name. Don't you?"

"Elizabeth is a fine name, but I want a special name for you. A private one." Her towel-covered hand moved fiercely back and forth across the toe of the red loafer. The other loafer sat by her left knee, looking polished and perfect. Everything Karen owns has that same cared-for look. You can lend her anything and be sure it will be returned to you looking as good if not better than it did before. She says it comes of having very little when she was growing up. Her family didn't have two nickels to rub together and her clothes were always hand-me-downs. She has learned to be canny with money and conscientious about possessions.

A special name just for me. How sweet of her. I couldn't help grinning. "Want to do my shoes?"

She looked up at me, pursing her lips as she studied my face. "I'll do one pair."

I went down the hall and into our bedroom. Down on my hands and knees, peering into the darkness under the dresser, I had an idea. "You could call me Sweet Heart!" There they were, misshapen from years of wear, my favourites, the black boots.

"What did you say," I heard her shout.

I scrambled to my feet, holding the boots with one hand.

"You could call me Sweet Heart," I repeated as I walked into the kitchen, into the smell of shoe polish. I said it as two distinct words. Sweet Heart, my sweet sweet heart.

"No, not those," she said, laughing. "I should have known. They're beyond help, you know. You got your money's worth out of them, no doubt about it, but it's time to throw them out."

I held the boots against my chest. "Never!"

"Give them to me."

I placed my treasured ankle boots beside the red loafer. "You could call me Sweet Heart."

"No." She rejected it immediately. "Not darling or dear or lovie. I want a special name for you, not any old common endearment."

"It wouldn't be common coming from your lips."

Karen smiled at me. The lines at the outer corners of her eyes deepened. She winked.

I wondered if she meant a nickname? When I was little, a gang of boys in the higher grades used to call me Leaping Lizard. I hated it. But it doesn't sound so awful now. Leaping Lizard. It has an energetic sound to it. I was always a lively kid.

I hadn't thought about that in years. The boys did it to torment me. And I felt tormented. My best friend, Diane, used to tell me not to pay them any attention. But I've never been any good at ignoring things. I prefer to deal with whatever is happening.

I opened the chequebook and started paying the bills. My mother calls me Lizabeth when she's feeling affectionate. When she's annoyed, she calls me Elizabeth Anne. Middle names are handy that way, I've noticed, for dragging out displeasure.

I pushed the bills away and looked at Karen. Her curly red hair was a warmer shade of red than her new shoes. When I was growing up there were unwritten rules about certain things and one was that redheads couldn't wear red or pink or purple. Karen wears all those colours, sometimes at the same time. She looks gorgeous. She's always been a renegade. It's one of the things I love about her.

"Did you have a nickname when you were a kid?"

She laughed. "Oh yes. They called me Carrot Top. Not very original, were they." Her right hand was buried deep in one of my boots and she was dabbing dots of black cream here and there on the scruffy leather. "But that's not what I have in mind, you know. Not a nickname. I don't know what it is I want, but it'll come to me."

She rubbed the cream into the leather with smooth circular motions. Her nose was pointed downward and her lips were thin from concentration. I don't feel a need to have a special name for her. She is special, just as she is. I call her Karen and I am content.

"Sometimes they called me Red." She waved the boot at me. "I liked it until one day after school one of the older boys, I think he was in grade seven, said 'Hey Red. Wanna show me your other red hair!' Nine years old and already having to put up with sexual harassment. The little bastard. I hit him and made his nose bleed."

I waited and watched her. I can watch her for hours on end, the changing expressions of her face, every mood different from the other and each one there for me to see. I watch her forehead, the lines around her eyes, her nose, the shape of her mouth, the way she holds her chin. I listen to the tones in her voice. I am learning to identify each mood.

She looked up and caught me watching. She smiled. It was a shy what-are-you-looking-at smile. My heart ached with love.

"Why are you staring at me?"

"I can't help myself, Karen. You're gorgeous."

The lines across her forehead softened and she started buffing the black leather with a brush. "Uummm. I need a special name for you. Something between us, from me for you. Do you know what I mean?"

I shook my head. "Not exactly."

"Never mind. It'll come. I've planted the seed."

I envy that in her, the way she trusts herself. Occasionally she loses it. Or maybe it's more that from time to time her faith gets buried beneath all the crap that can clutter a life.

Like last Saturday when she got out of bed and said, "Why do you always do *that* ?" Her voice was sharp and tense, and there were dark smudges under her eyes.

"Do *what* ?" My voice was tight.

"TurntheTVonassoonasyougetoutofbed!" She
stood in the doorway, staring at the screen,
waving her hands in the direction of the
television screen. "How can you watch that
stupid thing!"

Oh oh. She was in a foul mood. It was going to
be one of those days. And I was powerless to do
anything about it. Or was I? Maybe if I put my
arms around her and kissed her ear, her voice
would turn warm and friendly. But maybe she
would pull away and frown at me. How could she
talk to me like that? I felt like telling her to piss
off. I watched her for a minute, debating what to
do. What I wanted to do, more than anything,
was love her.

"Karen, love of my life, I turn the t.v. on
because I am inviting the goddess, in her many
disguises, into our living room."

She chuckled and I knew there was hope for
the day. I went over and put my arms around her
and whispered, "What's wrong?"

She rested her cheek against mine. "Nothing. I
had a weird dream, that's all. I feel yucky."

"Would a hot bath wash away the yuckies?"

She sighed.

"I'll start the bath. While you're washing away
the yuckies, I'll sit in front of the t.v. and watch
for the goddess."

She hugged me and I knew the day would be
fine. And it was.

In bed now, my arms around her and her head
resting on my shoulder, I said, "Did I thank you
for polishing my boots this morning? They look
terrific, you know."

"You're welcome. I did my best. They're falling
apart and you should throw them out."

I chose to ignore her advice. "Remember last Saturday, when you got up feeling yucky?"

"Yes. You were patient with me."

"What was the awful dream that upset you?"

"I can't remember anymore."

"Isn't it strange how a dream can throw you off and haunt you for days."

"Uummm."

"I had an scary dream the other night. I was on a road and there were snakes on both sides. I'm terrified of snakes and there were snakes everywhere I looked. It was so scary that I woke myself up. I decided I had to go back to sleep and bring back the dream and kill the snakes."

"Did you?"

"I couldn't. I tried but there were too many of them. So I woke myself up again."

Karen took my hand and held it in both of hers. "You could have used your magical powers and turned the snakes to stone with a nod of your head."

"Karen! I never thought of that! I'll try it next time."

"What do you think the dream meant?"

I shrugged. "I don't know. Maybe it's because I'm worried about work. When my boss retires next month, I don't know who will replace him. If it's his daughter, that's all right. We get along. But I've heard he's trying to get his son to move back here and take over."

"His son is a snake?"

"I don't know. I don't know him. All kinds of rumours are going around. It seems a waste of energy to worry about it before it happens. It's just that everything's up in the air at work and everyone's edgy."

I was born in Kincardine in 1949, but have lived most of my life in Ottawa.

I work part-time to support myself and my writing. One of my dreams is to be able to write full-time, day after day. Over the years I have worked as a nurse, lab assistant, typist, cashier, book shop assistant, manager of a word processing service bureau, bookkeeper, and administrator. Since 1987, I have worked for a national association that lobbies for better child care.

During the summer of 1989, after living in apartments most of my life, my constant companion and I rented a Mediterranean-style house filled with round shapes. Our home is in the neighbourhood where I grew up and I am thrilled to be living here again. I grow tomatoes, impatiens and lobelia. I wish I could own this house and stay here for the rest of my days. (The income I earn from part-time work in traditionally female jobs does not allow me that luxury.) I would dig up our tiny backyard and grow all sorts of flowers.

Some of my short stories have appeared in Canadian and American anthologies, including *By Word of Mouth*, *Finding the Lesbians*, *Dykewords*, and *Lesbian Bedtime Stories II*. I am currently working on my first novel, a second collection of stories, and some essays.

Candis J. Graham

"I love you, Elizabeth."

"I love you," I responded, drawing her closer. "Have you found a name for me?"

"No, not yet. While you were doing the grocery list this afternoon I was studying your aura. It was a beautiful purplish-red and the name Magenta popped into my head."

"I like that."

"It does have a grand feel to it, doesn't it. A purple aura means spiritual power. Magenta."

"I like the way you say it. Say it again."

"Magenta," she whispered against my cheekbone.

"Yes, Karen?"

"You like it, don't you?"

"I do."

"Let me sleep on it and see how it feels in the morning."

"Good idea."

She kissed me. I kissed her back. Mouths meeting and opening to taste, tongues touching tongues and teeth and cheeks, mouth juices mingling. When she moved away I felt the emptiness swallow me.

"Sleep well. Sweet dreams," she whispered as she turned over.

I snuggled against her warm back. "Sweet dreams to you." Magenta. I liked the sound of the word in my mind, but it didn't feel like me. "Karen?"

"Uummm."

"I'm not Magenta. I don't want another name. I like Elizabeth."

"So do I."

"Couldn't you think of a regular endearment?"

"Like dear or honey?"

"Yes, something like that."

"Uummm."

"Sleep well and have sweet dreams, Karen."

"And you."

I adore the feel of her body against mine. I like to stretch full length along her, touching as much of her skin as possible. I wondered if she could feel the dampness in my pubic hair against her behind.

"Elizabeth, chère."

"Yes?"

"Do you like that?"

"Like what?"

"Chère." She turned over and crushed her breasts against mine. "Elizabeth, chère," she whispered, her warm breath caressing my cheek.

It sounded graceful and sweet. "I think I do. Let's try it out. You say it, then kiss me. Say it again and kiss me."